Deadly Oath

I0584696

By Wendell Peeples

Wendell Peeples

Deadly Oath

Manufactured in the United States of America
Peeples Publishing LLC
Detroit MI 48204

ISBN 978-0-578-35507-8

This book is dedicated to my family and friends, whose unwavering belief in me has been my anchor through every challenge and triumph. Your encouragement has fueled my determination, your patience has steadied my steps, and your faith in my dreams has carried me further than I ever imagined. From the quiet moments of reflection to the long nights of hard work, you have been there, reminding me why I write and who I write for. This journey is as much yours as it is mine, and I am forever grateful for your love and support.

—Wendell Peeples

Wendell Peeples

Prologue

For the past two weeks, the killer has worked the night shift at the plant. Standard gig—uniform, flashlight, log sheet, same loop every hour. But tonight feels different.

Angela stands in the booth, already on duty when Raymond arrives. She wears her usual sharp look—black pants, a white shirt, and a red-and-white patch on her shoulder, as if it means something. Run DMC blasts from her earbuds as she bobs her head to the beat.

Raymond walks past. He nods casually.

She barely glances up.

Good.

Raymond shows up right behind her, wearing that worn Detroit Lions shirt under his jacket like he wants people to know he is from here. We all are. But not all of us have a similar reason for being here tonight.

Unbeknownst to anyone, someone else joined the night shift two weeks ago. He is the real new guy—not listed on the payroll, not in the rotation, but always watching.

He installed three cameras. One inside the booth, another tucked in the factory's hallway, the third hidden in the locker room, low in the corner where shadows meet silence. He can see everything, hear everything—every step, every whisper.

And he is watching us.

He sits in the crawlspace with a tiny, battered TV tuned to the six-o'clock news. Flames tear through buildings downtown—Devil's Night is in full swing. But that isn't the fire that interests him. Now, his attention shifts to the factory's monitors. Angela steps out of the booth, crossing the lot toward the building. He switches feeds.

She slips into the locker room, where Raymond is waiting.

"Should we be doing this here? I feel like someone will find out," she whispers.

He hears everything.

Raymond chuckles, his voice low and dismissive. "You never questioned this before."

Angela pulls back, fumbling with her buttons. Her eyes dart toward the door.

"Is this right, or do you think we'll get exposed?" she asks, tucking her blouse back in.

He zooms in.

"I mean it, Ray. I don't feel safe here anymore," she mutters. "Not after what happened to that girl."

His posture stiffens.

"You mean Joyce?"

She nods. "You don't think it's weird how no one talks about her anymore? Like she never existed?"

Raymond rubs the back of his neck, glancing toward the door. "They said it was some drifter. Came in with a knife. Caught her alone in the boiler room."

Angela scoffs. "That's not what I heard. Her guts were removed. Like—scooped out."

I remember that part.

Raymond shakes his head. "It wasn't a knife. More like a... spear. Long. Precise."

Angela looks at him sharply. "No, no. They told me it was an axe. That her skull was split open down the center."

Raymond's voice drops, almost reverent. "No. It was clean. Almost surgical."

She hesitates in the doorway. Her fingers dip into her pocket. That's when she realizes something is missing— her earring. Her hand flies to her ear. She stiffens.

She hurries out of the locker room, down the hall, and back toward the booth. The killer adjusts the focus as she pulls out her phone. Her face tenses. She types a message. The reception is bad inside; everyone knows that—phones only work outside or on the higher floors.

Raymond grabs his flashlight and starts his rounds. His silhouette passes through beams of moonlight pouring through the upper windows. Forklifts cast jagged shadows across the walls. He lifts his phone, smirks, and snaps a selfie.

Then he sends it.

Angela receives it almost immediately, opens it, and enlarges it.

Her heart must've skipped.

"Who is that behind you, Raymond?" she texts.

He pauses when the message comes through and opens the photo again. There, just behind his shoulder— blurred, dark, wrong—is a shape. A figure.

He turns.

No one is there.

The phone rings.

"It looks like a coat on a rack," Raymond says, laughing nervously. "I didn't see anyone when I turned around. What did you need to talk to me about?"

"I lost my earring," Angela says. "If you come across it, put it in the booth drawer. Please let me know if you find it."

She is already in her car, tapping out another selfie. She sends it.

The killer hears all of it. He has the phone call on audio and the texts on screen. The photo Angela just sent glows on Raymond's screen. He nods and moves on.

Raymond starts his walk, as always. First checkpoint: the front door. He taps the wand on the metal ring. The wand buzzes and flashes blue.

Checkpoint confirmed.

He makes his way through the factory, arriving at the stairwell that leads up to the executive offices. Most nights he skips it, but tonight—maybe something feels off. Or perhaps he wants to prove something.

Step by step, he climbs.

He reaches the top. Quiet. Offices locked. The killer watches from the crawl space. Sees Raymond raise the wand again. He tapped again, and the wand flashed blue a second time.

Then Raymond turns and begins to descend the stairs.

He never makes it to the bottom.

The knife comes fast, sharp, and clean, straight into his chest.

Blood sprays the wall. His flashlight clatters against the concrete. He collapses to his knees.

Click-clack. The stairwell door slams shut in the distance.

He's gone before the blood finishes spilling.

Angela sits in her car, unaware, when her phone pings with a new message.

"Who is that in your back seat?"

She reads it once. Then again. Slowly, she raises her eyes to the rear-view mirror.

Her mouth opens.

She screams.

But no one hears her.

She thinks it over.

It isn't.

Not for Angela.

Chapter 1

I stand in front of the plant, trying to block out the sirens still echoing faintly from the earlier sweep. The crime scene tape flutters like a torn ribbon in the morning wind. My badge feels heavier than usual tonight. I don't sleep. Don't eat. Just replay the scene over and over in my head.

That's when I see it—the *Headline News* van pulling in, tires crunching against loose gravel like bones underfoot. The logo glares from the side of the truck, and I know right then the circus is about to begin.

Kristi Bell steps out first, her hair perfectly styled, as if she expects the spotlight. She wears a low-cut black dress and heels too high for a crime scene. But Kristi doesn't come to grieve—she comes to perform. Lucas, the cameraman, stays behind the wheel, his broad shoulders hunched forward like he knows how this will play out. He always does.

"Get the camera, hurry!" Kristi barks. Her voice cracks across the lot.

Lucas jumps into action while Kristi clutches her mic, flings open the door, and comes straight for me. I can already see the red record light blinking on the camera.

She doesn't wait. "This is Kristi Bell from *Headline News*," she announces breathlessly, "and standing next to me is Detective John Stanley of the Detroit Police. He has breaking information to share with the public."

She thrusts the mic toward me, eyes sharp and impatient. The camera lens feels like a barrel pointed at my face.

I clear my throat.

"Someone brutally murdered an employee inside this building... near the main staircase," I say, keeping my voice steady. His body was discovered by a fellow employee earlier this morning. The attacker didn't harm any other staff." The weapon may still be in the building."

Even as I speak, I know he is listening. Watching. Somewhere in the dark corners of this place, he is tuned in. I can feel it—like a breath against the back of my neck. Like we are both onstage, playing parts in a story only he knows the ending to.

Kristi turns slightly, listening to her earpiece. Then comes the voice from another anchor at the station— Norma. "Are there any witnesses, Kristi?"

8

She looks at me and says, "Here is the detective to answer that question."

I step into the frame again. "There is information we can't share at this time. However, I urge the public to remain vigilant. We're following leads. When we know more, you'll know more."

Kristi doesn't let up. "Are there any other details you can share, Detective? Anything the public should be concerned about?"

I meet her eyes. "We don't have that angle of the story yet. But trust me, we'll stay on top of it."

She gives a tight smile and turns to the camera. "Thank you, Detective. Back to you in the studio, Norma."

The red light on the camera fades, and silence returns.

But I know better.

The quiet means nothing. The killer is still out there—listening, just like he did when Angela and Raymond whispered in the locker room, just like he did when the camera caught something behind Raymond that wasn't supposed to be there.

Kristi walks off toward another shaken guard parked near the edge of the lot, her heels clicking like a metronome against the pavement.

I stand still. The silence presses in.

That's when my phone rings—sharp, jarring. I fumble to answer. "Stanley," I say, clearing my throat.

"John, it's me!" a voice shouts. It takes a second to register, but then I know—Andre, my partner from the police force. My best friend.

"What is it?" I ask, though, something in my gut already twists.

"It's about your nephew," he says. "It's Raymond. Last night was his shift."

My grip goes numb.

The crime scene. The blood on the steps. The security uniform.
No. God, no.

I turn toward the building, and my legs lock in place. I feel like a statue, waiting for lightning.

Behind me, I swear I feel eyes.

He is still watching.

Still close.
And now it is personal.

Chapter 2

floor the gas pedal, weaving through the morning traffic on I-94 like the city is burning behind me. Horns blare as I cut through lanes, my hands gripping the steering wheel tight enough to snap it. My Crown Vic groans with every hard turn, but I don't care. I have one mission: get to my family—fast.

There's a crash on the shoulder, a rear-end collision, and glass scatters like broken diamonds, but I can't stop. Not today. Not with what I have to say. I make the twenty-five-minute drive in fifteen.

As I pull into my mother's driveway, my heart thumps harder than the engine. Earth, Wind & Fire spills from the living-room window—"Reasons," I think. That's always my brother-in-law's favorite. Too cheerful for a day like this. Too normal.

I step onto the porch and hesitate.

The doorknob is cool in my hand. When I open it, the warmth of the living room slaps me in the face— familiar faces, forced smiles, all of them pretending they don't already know something is wrong.

I barely get through the doorway before my brother-in-law pulls me into a bear hug. His strength doesn't match the weakness in the room. Eyes dart to me like I carry death in my pockets.

They're right.

I step into the center of the room and take a deep breath. Eight a.m., and already the world feels off-balance.

"I know you've all been wondering what happened last night," I say, voice low. The words feel heavy. "There's no easy way to say this."

Every eye locks on me. My sister is already trembling.

"Raymond was murdered... at his job."

I don't know if someone screams first or if the sound comes all at once—gasps, cries, the soft thump of my sister's knees giving out as she collapses onto the sofa—her face crumples, buried in her hands.

Her husband—Raymond's father—grabs me and holds onto me like I'm the only thing keeping him from falling apart. His tears soak through my shirt. I don't move. I can't.

I swallow hard. "I don't know all the details yet. We're still piecing it together at the scene. But it's been all over the news since it happened."

Mom sits in stunned silence. I bend down and wrap my arms around her frail shoulders. Her eyes meet mine—glassy, distant—but she doesn't say a word.

Then Iris stands up, slowly. She approaches me, moving as if her bones might shatter with each step, and when she reaches me, she hugs me tighter than she ever has in her life.

Iris is my sister—the woman who raised Raymond. She molds him, loves him, and protects him as best she can. And now she's holding onto me because I'm all she has left to do the one thing she can't: get justice.

We sit at the dining-room table, and Iris, just like we used to when we were kids. Back then, we could talk about anything. But today? Words feel like landmines.

"John... you and Raymond are close," she says. Her voice cracks on his name. "I'm gonna miss that uncle-nephew bond you two have."

I nod, but I can't speak. If I open my mouth, I'm not sure what will come out.

She takes a deep breath and wipes her eyes. "How's everything been around your way?"

I welcome the question like a lifeline. "Same old mess. People are still speeding up and down the street with all that loud-ass music. Kids wildin' out like they don't have homes to go to." Iris chuckles through her tears.

"These boys come over here and do all the dumb shit they're too scared to do at home."

"Tell me about it," I say, laughing with her for the first time in what feels like years. "I thought moving in with me would have saved you from all that."

"For a minute there, I believe it," she says, cracking the faintest smile.

That smile—that tiny sliver of who she used to be—is everything.

"It's good to see you laugh," I tell her. "That's the Iris I know. We're gonna get through this. You and me. Together."

She leans her head on my shoulder. "Thank you. But do me one favor?"

"Anything. You name it."

"My co-workers always call me Stanley," I respond. "But to the people I love? I only want to hear John."

I pull her in closer. "You got it."

She pulls away slightly, her eyes locking with mine, pleading, burning with something more profound than grief.

"Find out who killed my baby," she says, her voice nearly a whisper, like it hurts even to let the words out.

Tears roll down her face. I can feel her shaking.

I hold her close, steady, and lean in.

"I will," I whisper. "I swear to God, Iris... I will."

And in the back of my mind, I know he's still out there.

Listening.

Waiting.

And when I find him, he'll learn what it means to cross a Stanley.

Or maybe.

Maybe he already knows.

Chapter 3

The killer slips the knife into the backseat—right beneath the folded blanket, just in case. It's wiped clean, of course. No sense in getting sentimental about things like that. The blade has done its job. Swift. Quiet. Efficient. But now he has places to be.

He leans against the door for a moment, breathing in the stillness of the morning. There's a long drive ahead, and he wants to arrive early. Today isn't just any day.

Today, he'll see Angela.

He smiles without meaning to—just a twitch of the lips that spreads like a ripple in still water. Angela. She'll be at the job fair, sharp in her corporate armor, scouting fresh talent for her Fortune 500 overlords. He wonders if she'll recognize him immediately. They haven't spoken in a while, but you don't forget someone like him. Not really.

He shuts the car door gently and walks back inside. His suit jacket still hangs in the closet, and his résumé sits neatly printed on the kitchen table. Presentation matters. Always does.

The TV is still on, murmuring from the corner of the room. He pauses when he hears his name.

Stanley.

He turns to the screen, and there he is—Detective John Stanley, standing in front of a sea of flashing cameras, the press eating up every pained breath like it's gospel. He clenches his jaw, but his voice trembles beneath the surface.

"I've just found out that the man murdered at Ring Zone is my nephew," I say, choking on the last word. "If there's anyone with information... please... contact the number at the bottom of your screen."

His eyes are bloodshot. He looks like he hasn't slept. Grief ages him overnight. The killer tilts his head, studying him like a painting.

Good. Let it eat you alive.

The screen flickers to a picture of the factory—gray walls, rusted pipes, lifeless windows. Then they cut to some nearby train tracks. The killer remembers those tracks. He crosses them the night it happens, just before the rain starts.

"Kristi, have there been any new clues in the case? Does Detective Stanley know why this happened?" the anchor asks as the camera zooms in on her.

Kristi Bell. Gorgeous. Professional. Practically shaking from the proximity to real tragedy.

"The detective had to identify his nephew's body early this morning," she says solemnly. "The investigation is just beginning. Back to you, Roger."

And just like that, they move on. Some puff piece about a kitten stuck in a drain.

He clicks off the television.

His heart is steady. Calm.

Stanley doesn't know. Not yet. He's still searching in the dark, grasping at shadows.

But he's already two steps ahead.

He gathers his papers, buttons his shirt, and slides on his jacket. Last check: keys, wallet, blade. The house is silent, still smelling faintly of bleach. He locks the door behind him, twisting the deadbolt slowly and precisely, then pulls it shut with a loud slam that echoes down the street.

The engine rumbles to life. He shifts into gear.

Lawrence Tech, here he comes.

And Angela?

She has no idea what awaits her.

Chapter 4

I spend the next hour looking through statements from employees at the factory. Most of them found out about the murder when it splashed across the morning news—Raymond's face, the blood-streaked floor, and my voice cracking on live television.

When I'm done, I catch sight of her.

Mona.

An older woman, possibly in her late 50s, is being led into the precinct in handcuffs. Her blouse is knotted up just beneath her chest, and her denim skirt barely covers her thighs. The same hot mess she always is.

"Damn bitch! Motherfucker!" she mumbles under her breath as she staggers in the door of the precinct.

"You just can't stay out of trouble, can you, Mona?" I say, already exhausted by the sight of her.

"I guess not! Does that answer your question, Detective?" she spits, flashing that defiant smirk I've seen too many times before.

"I didn't do anything wrong, Detective. Let me go," she adds.

I cross my arms and stare at her.

"I've heard that one before. Over and over. I gave you a break the first time. Even the second. But this time? You're not slipping through."

She rolls her eyes like she's bored with her own life.

Moments later, I am back at my desk. I dial her son, Robert, to let him know his mother **is** cooling off in a cell again.

"What did she do now, Detective?" he snaps, clearly used to these calls.

"I'll tell you when you get here," I reply and hang up before I lose my patience.

Mona is a side distraction—one I don't need today, not with Raymond's blood still haunting the edges of my thoughts.

I lean back in my chair, scrolling through news footage, interviews, and articles. People constantly repeat the same damn thing when someone takes a loved one: He was an angel. He had no enemies.

I want to believe that about Raymond.

But death has a way of pulling skeletons out of closets.

He takes that security job to make some money. Nothing more. No one thinks it'll cost him his life. I pull out the photos from the scene again, my stomach tightening the moment I see him—face down in a pool of blood—his badge still clipped to his shirt. The area around the stairwell is narrow. Cramped. Just a flight of stairs tucked beside a blank wall. No place to hide.

So, how the hell does someone get close enough to kill him?

I pick up the phone and call Betsy, the woman in charge of hiring the security firm for the factory. The moment she answers, I hear the smugness oozing through the receiver.

"Betsy, I've got a few questions."

"Oh, Detective," she says with a dramatic sigh. "The guards at Ring Zone work eight-hour shifts. Three of them total, over a twenty-four-hour period. When I work that shift, I'm so sleepy that I barely make it through. But here, the company terminates anyone caught sleeping on the job."

I can feel the headache already blooming behind my eyes.

"One more thing—who's assigned the guards to the midnight shift on the night of the murder?"

"I wouldn't know," she says quickly. "There's another person in charge of that. I'll email you the supervisor's name. He'll have the full roster."

Of course, she passes the buck. I hang up, teeth clenched. My inbox pings a few minutes later. The list of guards arrives.

I scroll through the names, skimming until one name stops me cold.

Robert.

I stare at it. Can't move for a second. Robert. Mona's son. The same Robert who's now waiting in the front lobby.

Is it just a coincidence?

My pulse quickens. I stand, slip the folder under my arm, and walk out to greet Robert.

He stands at least 5'11", hair clipped close to his scalp, clean-shaven, casual. He looks me in the eye and shakes my hand. No hesitation.

"Come with me," I say, keeping my voice neutral.

In my office, I offer him a seat. He takes it without a word.

"How long have you worked at Ring Zone, Robert?"

"About six months," he replies easily. "I mostly work overnights. I've relieved Raymond plenty of times. I knew him. Everyone did, but I didn't work that night."

He doesn't flinch. Doesn't stutter.

I ask if he knows anything about the murder.

"Heard about it on the news," he says, "just like everyone else. I don't know who'd do something like that.

Maybe talk to the other guards—someone else might've seen something."

I nod. "We'll stay in touch."

He leaves just as calm as he enters.

I'm not sure what to make of it. Yet.

Mona joins her son in the lobby. She doesn't say a word. Neither does Robert. They leave together, the doors swinging shut behind them.

I sit back down at my desk, my gut coiled tight. Something doesn't feel right.

Then the phone rings. The woman's voice on the other end is trembling, barely above a whisper.

"I have information about the case," she says.

My breath catches.

"Can you meet in person?" I ask.

She gives me an address, a number, and one name: Lexi.

Before hanging up, she says something that sends a chill down my spine.

"I know someone who's involved—and they're a lot closer to you than you realize.".

Chapter 5

I am parked in front of Lexi's house in ten minutes flat**,** engine still ticking hot. My fingers tap the steering wheel. There's something about the tremble in her voice over the phone, the urgency. I don't like it.

She's already at the door when I step out of the cruiser—waiting, eyes darting between the porch light and my badge.

"Lexi," I say, flashing my ID. "I'm Detective Stanley."

"Please come in," she says, her voice low. "I'm sorry for the short notice, but... I had to talk to you."

She shuts the door behind me, and immediately the scent of brewed coffee and lavender candles hits my nose.

Her place is small but warm. Lived-in. The kind of space where secrets don't stay quiet for long.

"I understand you have some information to share?"

She nods, but her eyes drift over to the wall, lined with framed photographs of R & B icons from the '80s and '90s.

"You a Prince fan?" I ask, trying to break the ice.

"Since I was fifteen," she says with a faint smile. "Most of those are signed. I **got** to meet a few after the concerts**,** good memories."

I nod, appreciating the moment, but I'm not here for nostalgia.

"Lexi... I need you to start from the beginning. And if it's okay with you, I'd like to record our conversation."

"Yes," she says, folding her hands in her lap. "Go ahead."

I hit the record button and lean forward.

"I get a call from my friend Mia," she says, reaching for her mug. Her hands shake slightly. "She **tells** me her ex-boyfriend... he's being looked at as a person of interest in Raymond's murder."

I pause, letting the words sink in.

"Her ex-boyfriend? What's his name?"

"Dominic. And apparently, the cops think he had a grudge against Raymond."

That makes no damn sense.

"Hold on," I say, narrowing my eyes. "How would Dominic even know Raymond? What's the connection?"

Before she can answer, a noise rings out from the back room—a voice. A woman crying.

Lexi shoots up. "Sorry—I left the TV on in the bedroom. I'll turn it off."

I listen closely. The newscaster is covering the case again. My case. Raymond's murder. They're showing the factory, my face, me begging for leads.

She returns a moment later, brushing a strand of hair behind her ear.

"How did you hear about the murder at Ring Zone?" I ask.

"I told you... Mia told me. And she also told me that the guy who got killed was your nephew." She shakes her head, angry now. "This whole thing is twisted. It doesn't make any damn sense. I hope they find who did this."

Her voice cracks with rage—or maybe guilt.

"Lexi," I say gently, "thank you for being honest. Now tell me about Mia and Dominic. What was their relationship like?"

She doesn't speak—just reaches for a photo album sitting on the table beside her. She flips it open and holds up a photo.

"Mia and Dominic. That's them at a nightclub. She's sitting on his lap. I remember this night, December. I helped her pick out that outfit."

I study the man's face—Dominic. Young. Sharp features. Clean-cut. Nothing remarkable. But something about his eyes—it feels familiar.

"And their relationship?" I ask.

"They had their ups and downs like anyone else," she says with a shrug. "Mia never said much. Not to me."

She flips the page. "This one—Dominic just **got** off work. He **works** in security. Southfield. That's his uniform—black pants, white shirt."

I lean in; I can't make out the name on his badge.

"What company **is** it?"

"Caught Security, "I took that photo three weeks ago," she says.

My stomach drops.

Caught Security.

"That's the same company Raymond **worked** for," I mutter, my eyes locking on hers.

She looks away.

When she turns back, tears well in her eyes, she places her trembling hands on her lap and whispers, "Detective... Dominic is my cousin."

And just like that, the room turns ice cold.

Chapter 6

I find Dominic behind the science building at Dearborn College, sweeping the walkway with a long-handled broom like the weight of the world is in the bristles. The sun dips low, casting long shadows across the concrete. He looks up and spots me approaching, and his eyes narrow.

"Dominic West?" I ask.

He gives a nod, then leans the broom against the wall and wipes his hands on his jeans. "Yeah. That's me."

"I'm Detective Stanley. Appreciate you taking the time."

We shake hands, his grip firm but guarded. I can already feel the tension simmering beneath his skin. He isn't a man excited to be helpful—this is a man on edge.

"I'm following up on a murder. Big case. Been all over the news." I keep my tone steady, but my eyes never leave his.

Dominic sits on the bench near the building entrance, legs spread wide, back stiff. "Someone already called me about this, detective. I ain't got nothing to do with that crap."

His voice cracks a little, but not from fear. It's defensiveness. Guilt maybe. Or just a man used to being accused.

"We're investigating the homicide at Ring Zone. Your name came up. Did you work there?"

"I was there for maybe a week. A week and a half tops. Then I got moved to another site."

"You hear anything? See anything strange? Know the victim? Raymond Stanley?"

"Nah," Dominic says, shaking his head. "I didn't know the dude. He took over my shift after I left. Some guy who floats from site to site trained me. His name was Shawn or Robert. But me? I never met Raymond. I ain't in this mess, Detective. You got the wrong guy."

He raises both hands like I'm already cuffing him.

I study him. Tall, wiry, worn t-shirt clinging to his chest. No visible injuries. No bruises or cuts on his arms or knuckles. But something about his story feels off. Clean. Too clean.

People lie. They lie with their mouths while their eyes twitch and their hands tremble. But Dominic? He's calm. Controlled. Almost like he rehearsed this.

Still, one detail sticks out—Shawn. The name matches someone already on my radar. And if Dominic is right, Shawn trained Raymond. That makes him more than a footnote.

I hand Dominic my card. "If anything else comes to mind, call me."

He nods but says nothing. I turn and walk back to my cruiser, my brain already cycling through a dozen questions. Something isn't adding up.

The drive to the technology building is short, but my thoughts are anything but calm. By the time I reach my office, I've already pulled up Shawn's file. His name has come up before, buried in a stack of employment rosters from the security firm. Student. Guard. Accounting major.

And he just so happens to be on campus today.

Lucky me.

I make my way to his classroom, standing just outside the door. Mr. Mayes is handing out test results and throwing compliments like confetti. "Good work, everyone! Solid scores this time!" His voice is cheerful, a little too cheerful for a day like this.

Shawn sits in the second row. Light-skinned. About 5'7". Wearing a bright blue college shirt and a fake smile, like it's part of his uniform. The kind of guy who makes friends fast and hides secrets faster.

He laughs at a joke, leans over to whisper something to the student next to him—Robert, I realize—the same Robert who bailed out Mona, and the same Robert who conveniently worked at Ring Zone.

Now they're all here. All connected. And all pretending they're not.

Then I hear Shawn say something that freezes the blood in my veins.

"I still can't believe Raymond's gone. I trained him, man, at that location on Wayne Road. I was the last person to show him the ropes. Now this? No break-in, no nothing. Shit's got me watching my back."

My heart thuds against my ribs. So Shawn does know Raymond. And he trained him. That detail alone changes everything.

I knock once on the glass and wait for him to look up.

"Shawn," I call. He turns, the easygoing look on his face vanishing the moment he sees my badge.

"Detective Stanley," I say, stepping into the doorway. "We need to talk."

The room goes quiet. Shawn freezes. His friends look away.

But Shawn, he doesn't move. Doesn't say a word.

Just stares at me.

And in that moment, I see it—the flicker of recognition and fear.

Before I can speak again, Shawn stands up.

"I... uh... gotta grab something from my car real quick," he mumbles.

And then he bolts.

Out the back.

Gone.

"Shawn!" I shout, but he's already halfway down the hallway, pushing through the back exit like a man on fire.

I take off after him.

My shoes pound against the tiled floor, echoing through the narrow corridor as students turn to look at me. I burst through the back doors just in time to see him sprinting across the parking lot, weaving between cars like he knows exactly where to go.

Guilty. Shawn's running because he knows something. Or worse—he did something.

I yank open my car door and throw it in drive, tires squealing as I shoot out of the lot and round the corner. He's fast—faster than I expect—but I cut him off at the edge of the science wing.

He skids to a stop, looks around like a cornered animal, then darts between two dumpsters.

I jump out of the car.

"Shawn, stop! Don't make this worse than it already is!"

He doesn't stop.

He disappears behind the building, and I follow. The stench of old food and grease hits me like a wave, but I keep moving. My hand hovers over my holster, just in case.

I turn the corner and find him standing dead still.

He raises his hands. His chest heaves.

But he's not looking at me.

He's staring at something behind the dumpster.

I step forward slowly, angling my body to the side. "What is it, Shawn?"

He turns, wide-eyed, and whispers, "I didn't know... I didn't know it was gonna go this far."

"What are you talking about?" I ask, stepping closer.

Then I see it.

A black duffel bag. Torn open. Inside—blood-soaked clothes. A shattered phone. And a name tag that reads:

Raymond Stanley.

My stomach drops.

I reach for my radio to call it in, but then—

A metallic click.

I turn.

And someone is behind us.

Holding a gun.

"Back away from the bag," the voice says coldly.

Shawn's face goes pale. My hand freezes over the radio. The figure steps into the light, but I can't see their face—just the barrel of the gun and the glint of something metallic on their wrist.

A watch.

The same kind Raymond wore the night he died.

I lock eyes with the figure and say, "Put the weapon down."

But they don't.

They smile.

And then—

BANG.

Chapter 7

The shot rings out like a whipcrack. I dive behind the dumpster, dragging Shawn down with me as the bullet slams into the metal above our heads. Sparks fly, and my heart thunders like a war drum in my chest.

Shawn shakes beside me, lips quivering. "Oh my God... oh my God..."

"Stay down," I growl, pulling my weapon.

I peek around the corner.
No one.
Just the flutter of a plastic bag in the wind. The alley is empty.

But that can't be. I just saw the shooter.

"Don't move," I whisper to Shawn, and creep forward, my steps light, my senses wired.

The alley twists sharply around a brick wall—perfect for someone to duck into.
I turn it quickly, gun up.

Nothing.

Just an open gate swinging on rusty hinges and the sound of tires screeching in the distance.

Whoever fired that shot—they vanished.

I rush back to Shawn. He's curled into himself, staring at the bag like it might explode.

"You okay?" I ask, patting him down for blood. "Did you get hit?"

He shakes his head, still dazed. "No, no, I'm fine... but that bag... those clothes... that's his stuff. That's Raymond's. I swear to God I didn't know—"

"I believe you," I say, though I don't know if I do. "But you're going to need to come down to the station."

"I didn't kill him," Shawn blurts out. "But I know who might've. That guy, Dominic, wasn't alone at the site that night."

My jaw tightens. "What do you mean?"

Shawn looks up at me with glassy eyes.

"There was someone else. A floater—worked random shifts, didn't clock in right. Nobody paid attention to him because he was quiet and didn't talk much. But Dominic said the guy watched people."

"Watched?" I ask, narrowing my eyes.

"Yeah," Shawn whispers. "Watched like he was studying them. Like he was waiting."

I feel something cold slide down my spine.

The shooter didn't want the bag found.
Raymond's name tag.
His blood.

I reach for my phone to call backup, but just as I do—
It vibrates.

A new message.
No caller ID.

Just one line:
"Detective Stanley, stop digging. Or you're next."

Chapter 8

The message on my phone burns like a brand. "Detective Stanley, stop digging. Or you're next."
No name. No number. Just a warning typed by someone who knows how to cover their tracks.

I turn the screen toward Shawn.
"Does this message look familiar?"
He glances at it, face pale. "It's blocked."
"That wasn't the question."
He swallows hard. "No, it doesn't. I swear."

He's not lying. Or if he is, he's damn good at it. But my instincts tell me the real liar is still out there—watching us, probably from across the street or some rooftop. I can feel it—a tightness in my neck, like eyes drilling into the back of my skull.

Someone doesn't want me getting closer.

Too bad.

I slide the phone into my pocket. "Let's go. You're not walking out of here until I figure out why someone wants you dead, too."

We reach the cruiser in silence. I open the door for Shawn, but before he gets in, he turns to me, trembling.

"There's something I didn't tell you."
I freeze. "Talk."

"The floater. The guy Dominic mentioned—the quiet one? I only heard his name once. Some guards called him Sam. Just Sam. But the way they said it, it was like they were afraid of him. Like he wasn't one of them."

Sam.

That name hits me like a punch to the gut.
It was in Raymond's final report—the name of a guard who never clocks out but somehow always shows up on the shift sheets.

A ghost in the system.

I clench my jaw. "Get in the car."

As I pull away from the curb, I glance in the rearview mirror.
A black sedan sits parked two cars behind us. Tinted windows. No license plate.
It pulls away when I do.

Someone is following us.

"Hold on," I mutter, taking a sharp left and speeding through a yellow light. The sedan follows, slow and steady, like it doesn't want to be obvious, but not too far behind.

Shawn notices it too.
"Is that—?"
"I see it."

I reach under my seat and grip my backup Glock.

The car behind us suddenly swerves down an alley and vanishes.

Coward.
Or worse—they were watching to see where we'd go.

I drop Shawn off at the precinct and instruct two officers to hold him until I say otherwise. No phone. No visitors.

When I step back outside, the sky is darkening. Rain threatens overhead, and the air is thick with a storm that hasn't broken yet.

I light a cigarette with a shaking hand, staring at the phone in my palm.

Sam.

Why does that name sound so damn familiar?

Then I remember something from Raymond's file. A transfer slip—barely legible, scribbled over with two signatures.
One is Shawn's.
The other—Sam F.

Deadly Oath

I dash inside, heart pounding, and pull up the employee log from Ring Zone. I scan the records until my eyes lock on the name.

Samuel Freeman.

Address: unknown.
Phone: deactivated.
Emergency contact: none.

No digital footprint. No history. No ID on file except a blurry badge photo...

And that face
I lean closer to the screen, heart dropping into my stomach.

I've seen that face before.
At the funeral.
He stood in the back row. Sunglasses on. Head bowed. Not a single tear.

I blink, and the image burns into my mind.

He was there. Watching.
And now—
He's hunting me.

Chapter 9

I can listen to Kayla talk all day. There's something about her voice—soft, sure, and full of insight. She's like a breeze cutting through the stale air of my life. A breath of clarity. Of truth. She loves me, I think, in that quiet, complicated way people do when they've seen you fall and still stick around.

I haven't looked for a job in years. Don't want to. Can't stomach the thought of going back into that jungle. I've already been chewed up and spat out once.

"John, are you even listening to me?" Kayla's voice cracks through my thoughts, sharper now, irritated.

"Sorry, Kayla," I say quickly. "Sometimes I get lost in the story. Go on."

She sighs but smiles through it. "Like I was saying...
You need to dress like you're interviewing for a job. I
taught algebra at the university, remember? Shawn was
one of my students. He used to hang out with those three
guys—always stuck together. I don't know if they were
real friends or just convenient ones, but today? They've
been moving from table to table here at the fair, trying to
land something. The problem is they suck at it. Their
interview skills are a mess."

I lean in. "Did you notice anything... off?"

"Not really. Just the usual nerves and poor prep. I
know Shawn, though. He's just trying to land a job like the
rest of them."

She glances over my shoulder and stiffens slightly.
"I've gotta head back to my table. I'll call you later. Maybe
dinner after this, if you're up for it."

I nod, distracted because I see one person of interest.

Robert.

Standing in line again. I can't believe it.

He doesn't know I'm watching. Doesn't know that
Dominic named him—Robert—as the guard who trained
Raymond, my nephew—the same nephew who turned up
dead.

I have to move now. Quietly. I slip into line,
pretending to be just another desperate job seeker. My
heart thuds like a war drum in my chest. I'm close. Too
close to mess this up.

The recruiter at the table is a sharp-looking redhead, dressed in a gray suit, pearls gleaming at her throat. Robert hands her his resume.

"Good morning," he says.

"Good morning," she answers, all business.

"What position are you interested in?" she asks.

"Payroll," Robert replies confidently. "Used ADP in my last role."

They exchange formalities, but it's clear—she's not impressed. When Robert admits he hasn't done manual payroll taxes, her polite façade slips.

"Thank you for applying," she says flatly. "Next."

I watch his shoulders sink as he steps aside. I hate how these recruiters operate. I've seen too many brothers shut out for the way they talk, walk, or don't fit a mold.

I approach him casually. "Robert," I say, nodding to him, "I spoke with you earlier."

The others join in. I recognize their names from my list. Each man has a connection to the plant. Each one ties directly to the case..

"I am Detective Stanley. I am investigating Raymond's murder."

They tense. I keep it cool.

"Just need a quick hand raise," I say. "Who trained Raymond?"

Robert hesitates, then lifts his hand slowly.

Bingo.

"You remember anything about that night, Robert?"

He scratches his temple. "It rained that morning. I remember that because I had to drop off checks. I was the site supervisor back then—making sure everything ran smooth."

I nod. "Thanks. Just one more thing."

I lean in, lowering my voice. "At the crime scene, we find boot prints—lots of them. Lab matches them to a specific style. Size eleven. Only sold at three stores in the city."

Robert stiffens. His eyes flick to the others, then back to me.

I watch him swallow.

Because I haven't finished.

"We pull the purchase records," I say, voice calm but cold.

"And one person bought that exact size the day before someone murdered Raymond."

Robert takes a step back.

And then—

I see him run.

Chapter 10

I don't hesitate. As soon as Robert bolts, I tear out of the line after him, ignoring the startled faces around me. Papers fly, resumes scatter to the ground, and I hear the redhead recruiter gasp as I shove past her table.

"Robert!" I shout, but he doesn't stop.

The job fair is busy—tables, people, banners, and folding chairs. He weaves through them like he knows the place inside out. But I'm faster. More determined. I don't need to see the layout. I need to catch him before he vanishes for good.

He pushes through a side door near the loading dock—an emergency exit. The alarm screams as it swings open, but no one follows us out. It's just me and him now.

The air outside is thick and damp. The morning rain still clings to the pavement in slick patches, and the sky hangs gray and heavy like it knows what's about to happen. I sprint after him, my coat flapping behind me, my shoes pounding against the ground.

I'm closing in.

"Robert, stop! You run now, and I will assume you have something to hide!"

He doesn't even look back.

That's all the confirmation I need.

My hand grazes the edge of my badge, but I don't pull it out yet. Not while I'm still trying to keep this from turning into something worse.

Robert cuts through a narrow alley between two warehouse buildings. Trash cans, loose crates, and broken pallets clutter the path. He knocks one over behind him, trying to slow me down, but I jump over it, nearly slipping on the wet cement.

That's when I see it.

He ducks through a rusted metal door left cracked open. I follow without thinking, and everything goes dark.

Pitch black.

The door slams behind me.

I pause. My breathing is loud now. Heavy.

Something isn't right.

I reach for my flashlight. The beam cuts through the darkness just enough to show I'm in an abandoned shipping room. Boxes stacked to the ceiling. It smells of oil, dust, and something else, something faintly metallic.

I move slowly, my heart thudding in my ears. The silence is suffocating. And then—

A floorboard creaks.

I spin toward the sound, flashlight shaking slightly.

"Robert?" I call out.

No response.

Another sound—this time behind me. Fast. Like someone—or something—moving.

I turn again, but it's too late.

A shadow lunges.

Everything goes black.

Chapter 11

The hibachi shrimp sizzles on the plate in front of me, steam curling upward like whispers in the air. I'm seated near the window at a quiet Japanese spot on Hubbard Drive. The calm before the storm.

"You looking for a new job, John? It looks like it after I pulled you out of that warehouse," a familiar voice laughed from behind me.

I turn to see Andre—still broad-shouldered, still grinning like we're kids skipping class. I chuckle. "Naw, man. Just playing undercover again. You know how that is."

We both laugh, clinking our glasses like old times. We've been tight since high school—double dates, pranks, graduation—and somehow both ended up wearing badges. Life's weird like that.

But tonight isn't about nostalgia.

Andre gives me a once-over. "You in a suit and tie? Glasses too? You don't even need glasses."

"Props," I reply. "Trying to stand out. Blend into the job fair crowd, but not too much. Kayla told me the guys who worked with my nephew were there. Every one of them has Ring Zone listed on their resumes."

"Damn," he mutters. "You think one of them—"

"I don't think," I cut in. "I know. Kayla's the one who flagged their resumes. I've already talked to one of them—he wasn't working the night Raymond died. But there's another. I'm meeting him tonight."

I don't say more. The walls feel like they're listening. I hadn't expected to find them here—two women who look as polished as the lie they're selling. But there they are, seated at my table, sipping cocktails like they've earned a break from playing god with people's futures.

Cindy and Becky.

I've seen their names before—HR recruiters from the job fair. The same woman my nephew Raymond encountered before he ended up in a morgue drawer.

I shift in my seat, angled just right, the brim of my cap pulled low. To the big bosses, I'm just another job-hunting nobody grabbing dinner after a long day. But my ears are wide open.

"My feet are killing me," Cindy sighs, flicking a lighter and taking a long drag from a cigarette like it's some tranquilizer.

"Did you get many qualified candidates?" Becky asks, poking at a piece of hibachi chicken with her fork. She doesn't look tired—just annoyed.

Cindy scoffs. "Sure. Degrees, experience, all of it looked great on paper."

There's a pause—a crackle of tension.

"But?" Becky probes.

Cindy leans in, her tone sharpening into something colder. "They didn't fit our culture. I'm not about to pay twenty-seven dollars an hour for someone who might end up living next door to me."

I freeze. Not outwardly, but something in me turns to ice. That's not just corporate bias. That's something uglier. Deeper. And deadly familiar.

Becky doesn't even blink. Just nods, like she's heard it a hundred times.

"I gave the second interviews to others," she says quietly. "Ones that feel... safe."

Safe.

I know what that means--and they do too. Safe means familiar. Predictable. And, judging by the look in Cindy's eye, white.

The waiter drops the check on their table like a punctuation mark. There's a moment of awkward fumbling—Cindy checking her coat, Becky digging into her purse—before Becky sighs and pulls out her Visa.

"I'll pay," she says with a half-smile. "You can pay me back when we get to the car."

I watch them rise, walking toward the exit like nothing has happened. As if they haven't just betrayed every ideal their jobs are supposed to represent.

I finish my drink slowly and give them a head start. Then I pay in cash and slip out behind them, moving through shadows like a habit.

Becky parked across the street. I watch from behind a tree-lined alley as they laugh about the wallet Cindy has found on the backseat floor. Fifty bucks changes hands. The laughter fades.

Then they're gone, their car disappearing into the quiet blur of city lights.

But the storm hasn't passed.

No, it's only gathering.

And I'm right at the center of it.

I keep my eyes on them from behind. My instincts have started humming after what Kayla told me—too many of these hiring decisions are personal. Coded. And if these women are part of a larger network that keeps people like my nephew from rising, I need to know.

Cindy drops Becky off at her house—a quiet place on a tree-lined street. I wait until Becky goes inside before driving off. I have my next meeting lined up, but something nags at me.

A feeling I can't shake.

Hours pass.

My phone buzzes.

Kayla.

"She didn't answer," she says softly.

"Who?"

"Becky. I called to confirm our follow-up. It rang, then voicemail. I, I don't know why, but I feel like something's off."

I glance at the clock—three o'clock.

My gut twists.

"I just left her house. Can you call again?" I ask.

Kayla calls, still no answer.

I'm already turning the car around.

When I reach the neighborhood, everything looks still. Peaceful. I park down the street and walk up under the cover of night.

The porch light is still on. The door closed—no movement behind the glass.

I ring the bell.

Nothing.

Knock.

Still nothing.

A few seconds later, I hear a faint sound—a metallic clink, like something has dropped inside.

I reach for the doorknob.

It turns.

Unlocked.

I push it open slowly.

"Becky?" I call.

Silence.

The living room is dimly lit, illuminated only by the chandelier. Becky's purse is still on the table. Keys. Mail. A phone was vibrating on the hardwood floor.

Then I see it.

A single shoe.

Becky's.

Tipped over on its side in front of the stairs.

"Becky!" I shout, drawing my weapon as I move deeper into the house.

There's movement upstairs—a shadow. Something— or someone—is still inside.

I creep up the steps, every tread creaking beneath my weight. My breath slows. My grip tightens.

Halfway up, I hear it.

A low, ragged breath.

Right above me.

I turn the corner.

And that's when I see—

Chapter 12

I didn't expect much from the line at the party store on Livernois—just a bottle of ginger ale and a moment of peace. But then I heard the voices. Two women behind me weren't whispering or hiding, as if the world wasn't listening.

Angela. Fatima.

I knew the names from the job fair, especially Angela, who worked at Ring Zone. The company tied to Raymond's last paycheck and maybe his last breath.

I kept my eyes on the rack of gum and lottery tickets, pretending to be patient like the rest of the folks waiting in line. But my ears? Wide open.

They didn't notice me. They were too deep in it.

Angela was holding a bag of potato chips and sighing like the weight of the hiring process was too much for one soul to bear. "What did you think about the candidates today?" Fatima asked, her voice low and flat, like she was already exhausted by the answer.

Angela didn't miss a beat. "Some of them were solid. Degrees. Clean resumes. Steady jobs. But let me be real— we need some *brothers* in this organization. Not just the ones they parade around for photos once a year. Real ones."

There was a pause—a shifting of weight. I heard Angela take a breath like she was about to say something she shouldn't, but she said it anyway.

"I've worked damn near every low-paying job you can think of just to get here. It wasn't easy. And when I saw those resumes, some of them made me nervous."

Fatima made a sound. Could've been an agreement. It could've been discomfort.

Angela went on. "I know it's wrong, but if a guy I interviewed made me feel... threatened? He didn't get a second interview. I'm not setting myself up like that."

"Hmm," Fatima murmured.

Angela's tone dipped, bitter at the edges now. "Have you ever trained someone only for them to turn around and become your boss in less than a year? I have. Not again. These brothers want twenty-seven an hour? No way. I'm not pulling anyone into the company that'll leapfrog over me while I'm still trying to secure a raise."

I kept my posture still, eyes on the clerk who was scanning six-packs and swiping Lotto tickets. But my heart was ticking like a timer.

Fatima spoke next, a sharper edge to her words. "You know how this place works. They'll use you up, then bring in their cousin, neighbor, or the CEO's side chick and want *you* to train her. Then, when it's time for a raise? Suddenly, there's no budget."

She exhaled hard. "I gave the brothers second interviews, yeah—but none of them will get hired. They'll give the job to someone already inside. One of their 'safe picks.' Give them a quarter raise, pat them on the back, and keep the cycle rolling."

Angela laughed, but the sound was hollow. "Exactly. I want to protect my seat at the table. That's all."

The cashier waved me forward. I paid for my drink, slow and deliberate, then moved outside just as Angela and Fatima left the store, bags in hand, voices fading as they walked to their car.

I watched them from the corner of my eye. Angela fumbled with her keys, dropped them once, and found them buried beneath receipts and a mess of lip gloss. Fatima waited in the passenger seat, already scrolling through her phone like the conversation they'd had was nothing.

But it wasn't anything.

It was a glimpse into the rot.

Deadly Oath

I took a deep breath, gripping the steering wheel of my unmarked sedan. The sun was nearly down. The breeze had changed.

Something about the air told me this case wasn't cooling off—it was *just starting to burn.*

And next time
I wouldn't just be listening.
I'd be asking questions.

Chapter 13

t's just after 7:30 PM when the party starts popping. Cars line both sides of the street like a makeshift parade, engines still ticking hot as clusters of guests spill out, laughing and adjusting their clothes. Some wear tight dresses, others casual jeans—but everyone seems ready to forget whatever hell the week brought.

The bass throbs from inside the house like a pulse. House music. High tempo. Perfect for losing control. I keep a low profile, standing near the end of the block, leaning against a streetlamp like just another guy waiting for his ride. But I'm not here to party. I'm here to listen.

Wyatt's voice carries through the air—loud, cocky, and full of beer. "Man, this is what I've been waiting for. Time to live it up!"

"To success," Robert adds, and the others echo the toast. Glasses clink, and the crew scatters to the dance floor, their girls tugging them into the crowd like magnets pulling steel.

I take a slow walk up toward the house, keeping my badge and pistol tucked and my eyes open. I'm not going inside. Not yet. Something tells me the answers I need are out here, not in there.

That's when I spot two women sitting on their front porch. Both of them live next door to each other. One of them—Cindy—I recognize from a prior investigation involving housing complaints and anonymous reports. The other, Becky, I've seen before but can't place. I trail behind them at a distance, keeping my head down and my ears up.

They stop outside the door of their homes on the phone, laughing low and bitter like women who've seen too much and trusted too little.

"Can you believe this mess?" Cindy snaps from the chair on her front porch.

"Mess?" Becky asks, grabbing a small basket.

"They're throwing a damn party two doors from my house. And not just any party. One of those parties."

I slide into the backyard, pretending to browse while I lean closer to their voices.

"I told you," Cindy hisses, grabbing a soda from the fridge. "I didn't move into that neighborhood to deal with this kind of riffraff. That's why I screen my candidates like I do. I don't care how many degrees they have—if they don't fit, they don't get in."

Becky chuckles. "You're preaching to the choir. That's exactly why I nixed those two qualified guys from the interviews. One of them had a better résumé than mine,

"Exactly," Cindy scoffs. "We don't need that kind of shift. Our company, our culture."

My jaw tightens. I've heard enough. The discussion turned to qualified men—Black men—being denied work for no reason other than fear. Fear of being replaced. Fear of having to respect someone they never saw as an equal.

I step back toward the door when Cindy's voice drops.

"I don't care if that house is an Airbnb or not. I'm about to shut this whole thing down. I told you what happens when people like them move in."

A pause. Then: "Wait... Becky—did you hear that?"

Her voice shifts from smug to startled. I peek through the glass and see Cindy whip her head toward the front door. She looks shaken. Pale.

"I gotta go," she mutters, her hand shaking as she reaches for her phone. "Something's wrong. I think someone's in my house."

Before Becky can respond, Cindy darts out of her home.

I follow, keeping my distance.

Deadly Oath

She reaches her porch, keys trembling in her hand. She pushes the door open at Cindy's home, steps inside, and comes to a halt.

Then, I hear it.

A scream.

It echoes down the street—sharp, sudden, and bloodcurdling. Then silence.

I'm already sprinting toward the house, gun drawn, heart hammering like a warning drum.

But I'm too late.

By the time I reach the front door, the lights are out, and the only sound is the click-clack of footsteps disappearing into the dark.

Chapter 14

Andre and I sit posted up in my cruiser just off Woodward near 6 Mile, the red and blue strobe of the gas sign blinking like a slow warning. "Looks like the girls are out in force tonight," I muttered, drumming my fingers on the wheel.

"You catch them, we book them, then two days later, they're back out doing the same thing. It's a vicious damn cycle."

Andre adjusted his glasses and leaned back. "Some of them are on drugs, Stan. Some need the money. But this, this is one dangerous hustle to make a living."

Just as he said, we saw Brandy stomping down the sidewalk, her heels clicking like gunshots on concrete. "What do I look like, an ATM? Do I have ATM written across my damn forehead?" I heard her say. She snarled, brushing past a guy who got too fresh. She didn't even stop to look back—she was all fury and legs in that red mini.

In the parking lot, Dawn stood in front of the gas station, waiting—and fuming.

"You just put on my damn dress without asking?" Brandy shouted as she closed in. "You don't touch my shit!"

Dawn turned slowly, already pulling attitude like it was a second skin. "You wouldn't even know I had it on if you didn't come stomping up in here like a damn buffalo."

It escalated fast—too fast. Brandy threw the first swing. Then Dawn landed one of her own. We were out of the car the second we saw Brandy's wig tilt sideways.

"I'm looking at you, and you are enormous!" Brandy screeched. "You're stretching my dress out like a damn parachute! Talk to Jenny Craig!"

Dawn didn't flinch. She bent low, grabbed a brick off the edge of the sidewalk, and hurled it at Brandy's head.

The brick missed—but it didn't miss the gas station window. Glass exploded.

The alarm screamed.

I hit the lights.

They ran.

Andre and I gave chase, cutting down the alley between two shuttered buildings. They were fast, but we knew these streets better. We boxed them in behind a dumpster and a padlocked gate.

"Why were you two fighting?" I shouted, panting, pissed. "We've picked you both up more times than I can count. Over what time? A man? Money? Drugs?"

Brandy stood there, chest heaving, one heel broken and hanging on by hope. For a long time, neither said a word.

Then Brandy snapped, "Detective Stanley... she stole my dress. My favorite damn dress. Now look at it— stretched out like a body bag."

Andre let out an incredulous sigh. "A *dress*? You shattered a business window over a damn *dress*?"

"You're both responsible," he barked, grabbing Dawn's arm and snapping the cuffs on.

As we walked them back to the cruiser, I noticed something. Across the street, a car had pulled in and parked. But no one got out. Its headlights clicked off, but the silhouette of someone stayed behind the wheel. Watching.

From the other side of the vehicle, Brandy was still cursing under her breath as she slid into the back of the cruiser. "You know what? I hope your fat ass *never* fits into my clothes again."

Dawn just stared at her, eyes narrowed. Silent.

That's when Brandy looked past me, through the cracked glass of the storefront, and froze.

"What the hell...?"

I turned, instinct kicking in. A dark figure moved across the back lot, just past the broken window. It was subtle—too subtle for someone not trained to notice. But I did. A quick slink, like smoke with legs. One second it was there, the next—gone.

"John," Andre whispered, now at my side. "You saw that too, right?"

"I did," I said. "Let's move."

We got Brandy and Dawn secured. Then we peeled around the block, circling the lot.

Nothing.

Not a single trace of the figure. No footsteps. No sound.

Just the echo of Brandy and Dawn's fight—and the feeling that someone was listening just like I had been, hiding just out of reach.

I checked the rearview. Dawn's gold-trimmed dress glowed faintly under the dome light. Brandy sat next to her, arms crossed, still fuming. But neither spoke now.

We were all quiet.

Too quiet.

As we pulled onto the main road, I kept glancing at the side mirror. That figure didn't feel like a stranger. Something about it sent my stomach into knots.

"This wasn't just another fight," I said aloud, more to myself than Andre.

He looked at me. "You think someone else was watching?"

"No," I said.

"I think someone's *hunting*."

Chapter 15

The night air was thick, humid, with a hint of tension. Andre and I sat parked two houses down from a corner where we'd been tracking a few recent disturbances. My unmarked cruiser blended into the row of half-lit porches and cracked sidewalks.

Inside the car, the radio buzzed low. "You know," I said, tapping the steering wheel, "it's like a revolving damn door. We pick these girls up, book them, and within days they're back out like nothing happened."

Andre adjusted his glasses, peering out into the night. "Some of them are on drugs, John. Some are just trying to survive. It's easy to judge from the front seat of a cruiser. But out there—it's different. It's dangerous."

I didn't respond. My eyes were locked on Fatima and Angela pulling into a narrow driveway across the street in a silver Altima. I recognized them from an incident that occurred at a job fair last week. They'd both filed complaints, and something about them didn't sit right. Not wrong—just aware. As if they saw things that most people overlooked.

I reached over and hit the window button to lower it a bit. Just enough to catch their voices if the wind cooperated.

Fatima stepped out, already mid-sentence. "You know, I heard every word that recruiter said to those guys the other day."

Angela nodded. "That's why I switched spots at the booth. I needed you to see it, too—how she treated the African American candidates versus the others."

I leaned in slightly. My heart ticked up a beat. Idle gossip wasn't what I heard. The women were dissecting the kind of discrimination people like me were supposed to root out. And yet

"I interviewed with her once," Fatima said, her voice rising. "Didn't get hired. No surprise. But guess what? Now we work together."

Angela scoffed. "She always says, 'We need someone who fits the culture.' That's not code for experience. That's code for exclusion."

I glanced at Andre. He caught my look. We both knew this wasn't just a conversation—it was testimony.

But the shift came fast.

The deep roar of a Mustang's engine growled up the street—four men, tatted and shirtless, blasted by with their stereo pumping heavy bass and expletives. The women froze as the car tore past, and then Fatima sighed.

"To them, we're still just Black bodies. Doesn't matter what we wear or what degrees we hold."

Angela leaned on the steering wheel, jaw clenched. "Even in 2011, we're still told, 'You're not enough.' It's never about merit."

Andre whispered, "Damn..."

"They're right," I murmured. "They know exactly what's happening."

But then Fatima said something that made my stomach twist.

"You think what we did was any better?" Her voice cracked slightly.

Angela hesitated. "Could be seen that way."

What did they do?

I noted that for later.

They pulled into the driveway and climbed out of the car. I watched them separate toward their mailboxes—like clockwork. Routine. Nothing unusual, until Fatima looked over her shoulder. Her hand paused mid-motion. Angela noticed it, too.

"What is it?" she asked.

"Nothing. Thought I saw..." Fatima didn't finish.

I stiffened in my seat.

Across the street, the shadows moved.

It was slight. A dark figure shifting just beyond the fence line.

Andre straightened up. "You see that?"

"Yeah."

I dropped my hand to the door handle, but something stopped me. Instinct maybe. That shadow—it wasn't drunk. It wasn't high. It was *calculated*.

Angela and Fatima headed inside. I jotted a note on my pad: *Possible target. Suspect in proximity.*

From that moment on, everything seemed to happen in slow motion.

Fatima's light went on upstairs. Angela stayed downstairs. The neighborhood hummed with activity— kids still playing, a stereo somewhere playing '90s R&B— but there was tension in the air now. Static before the lightning.

I couldn't hear much after that, not from where we were parked. So we waited. I radioed in a possible prowler and stayed put.

Time passed.

Then I saw the flash of light from Angela's window— TV on, maybe. She emerged onto the porch, calling Fatima's name.

But no answer.

"Fatima, stop playing games," she yelled.

Andre and I were out of the cruiser now, walking slowly toward the house.

From inside came the faint sound of running, rapid footsteps on wood.

Then a scream.

Not a startled yelp.

A *blood-curdling scream.*

"Go! Now!" I shouted, drawing my weapon.

We reached the stairs just as Angela threw open the door.

"She's upstairs! Something's wrong!" she cried, eyes wide with terror.

I bounded up the stairs two at a time, gun raised, Andre at my back. The door at the top was ajar.

Blood.

It was everywhere.

Dripping from the walls, pooling on the floorboards. Fatima was nowhere to be found. Her house is ransacked, God.

"Clear the room!" I barked, heart thundering in my ears.

But whoever did this was already gone.

We made it to the back stairwell. Andre shouted, "There! Between the buildings!"

A shadow vanished into the night.

The only sound that remained was the echo of fleeing footsteps—click-clack, click-clack—getting fainter, swallowed by the darkness.

And just like that, the killer slipped away.

Chapter 16

I left Andre at Angela's home and circled the block, passed the old corner party store. Its neon sign buzzed, the lights chasing each other in a hypnotic loop like they were trying to run from something. The door swung open again and again—people shuffled in and out with plastic bags, eyes darting, nerves twitching.

Down the road, the CVS sign flickered once, then died. Right after, the party store's lights went black, too.

I didn't like it.

A group of men took off on foot. No hesitation. Something was up.

I threw on the red and blues, sirens howling through the night. Tires squealed. The cruiser jolted forward. They ran like hell—darting down a pitch-black alley. I followed fast, adrenaline kicking in. They vaulted a wall into a neighbor's backyard.

So did I.

The flashing lights turned the street into a twisted party of red and blue chaos. Everything felt too bright and too dark at the same time. My heart thundered in my chest.

I crashed into a house halfway through renovation— wood everywhere, old tarps, tools, the stench of mold and piss so strong it nearly gagged me. My gun drawn, the metal cool in my palm. I cleared room by room, clearing corners, checking closets, but the place was empty until I found a sign taped to a rotted door: "DANGER. KEEP OUT."

I moved anyway.

The hallway reeked. Water dripped from the ceiling in sluggish drops. Then—just as we were leaving—Angela appeared out of the darkness. She was running, gasping for air. Her nightgown clung to her legs, and her house shoes slapped against the pavement. A scarf was wrapped tight around her head, barely holding her hair back.

"Help me! Please!" she cried, voice cracked and desperate.

"What's the problem, Angela?" I asked, steady but alert.

She didn't answer, just pointed. "A woman... she's in trouble... please hurry!"

I followed her to a gray brick duplex where Andre met me. She motioned us around back. "You stay here," I told her. Andre and I moved up the stairs.

Then, something wet hit my cheek.

I paused. Reached up. Fingers came back slick and red.

Andre flicked his flashlight toward me. His face froze.

Angela screamed behind us and collapsed to her knees.

Blood. It was dripping onto me from the porch above. More than a little. A lot.

Andre followed the trail with his beam—blood seeping between the wooden planks above us. I looked at him. He looked at me. No words. We bolted up the stairs.

Guns drawn.

Back to the railing.

At the top of the landing, a woman was face down.

Angela's screams tore through the night. "IS IT HER!? Is it HER?!"

"Calm down," Andre said, kneeling next to the body. "We don't know who this is yet."

Angela pointed. "Her purse! It's in the dining room— on the table!"

Andre gently placed Angela in the back of the cruiser before jogging up the stairs again. He rifled through the bag, pulling out a license. Fatima Jones. Her face stared back at us in a DMV photo—calm, smiling, unaware. Pictures of her and Angela decorated the walls.

He looked at me and gave a slight nod.

Angela's wail was sharp enough to cut bone.

Andre called in backup, requesting EMS and the coroner. The street lit up with new units, their lights bouncing off brick walls. People spilled out of their homes, crowding the sidewalk. Among them was Kristi Bell, the raven-haired reporter in her signature black silk dress and too-red lipstick.

She wasted no time. "We are at the site of a murder—sources tell us the woman was well-liked in her community. No known enemies."

Her cameraman adjusted the light, and she gave us a full smile that didn't touch her eyes.

"Detectives, any comment?" she called out, mic already extended.

We ignored her.

"C'mon, boys," she said, moving closer. "Two tall, strong officers like you must know something. Whisper it to me. I can keep a secret."

The camera started rolling. "This is Kristi Bell, and I'm here with officers who've just made a disturbing discovery..."

I stepped in. "We found the victim at the scene. African-American female. No forced entry. Could've known her attacker."

"Is this a serial case?" she asked, the mic pushed under my chin.

"Too early to tell. But we're investigating all leads," I replied.

Once the broadcast wrapped, we pulled back and watched the crowd. Giant rats skittered across the alley. Kids still played in the street. It was midnight.

"Do you live here?" I asked a neighbor.

"Yeah," she shrugged. "But I wasn't home when all the yelling started."

Andre shook his head. "Different world. In our neighborhood, one loud car stereo gets a ticket. Here, they're used to chaos."

Sergeant Carl Smith showed up—tall, solid, a storm behind the eyes. "What do we have?"

"Fatima Jones. Recruiter. Late 40s. Multiple lacerations."

He nodded grimly.

We returned to the cruiser, but the night wasn't done with us.

Half a burger later, the radio crackled.

"All available units, east side. We need an immediate response."

Andre rolled his eyes. "Told you we wouldn't get to eat."

He slammed his drink down. Cola exploded everywhere—on the dash, on our uniforms. I smirked and smeared some on his cheek.

He blinked—then broke into laughter.

So did I.

Until the siren roared again and the streets turned into a blur.

At the new scene, the place was crawling with uniforms. A woman's body was found upstairs—cleaver in her skull, chest cut open. Blood had soaked the carpet.

A neighbor had requested a wellness check. She lived four doors down. The party is going on all night. No one heard a thing.

Andre shook his head. "Too neat. Too quiet. That's not right."

The coroner zipped up the bag. Another woman. Another unanswered question.

We made our way back to the cruiser, silent until Andre muttered, "You ever try to eat a steak after looking at a cleaver in someone's skull?"

"You forget," I said. "I almost became a mortician."

He barked a laugh. "And that's why you'll never enjoy fries again."

I punched him in the arm. He laughed harder.

Back at the station, Jenkins called us into his office. His voice was serious.

We braced ourselves.

Instead, he handed us a certificate—a commendation for taking down a serial killer last year. We'd done good work. He told us the mayor had arranged a banquet.

For a second, we stood there in stunned silence.

Then Carl peeked in with a knowing grin. "What's up, fellas?"

I'd never trust a moment of peace in this job. But that one, I let myself feel it.

For now.

Because somewhere in the dark, Sam was still out there. Watching. Planning.

And he wasn't done yet.

Chapter 17

The line outside Robert's party snakes down the block like it's a red-carpet event. Flashing lights, camera phones, heels clicking on the pavement—everybody wants in. The bass from inside is so heavy that it shakes the pavement under my boots. From this distance, the house looks like it's breathing.

Security's tight tonight. Derrick patting down Juan, who smiles like he owns the place. He nods at the guards and slides past them into the house. His crew's still outside getting checked. The crowd's thick and impatient. I can feel the heat rising off the bodies even out here.

I'm posted in the cut, watching from the shadows near the driveway. Uninvited. Unseen. I don't need to be on the list to do what I came to do.

The music inside swells—an old-school track drops, and the whole house roars. That's my cue.

But before I move, I spot Ian.

He's standing alone near the bushes, just outside the glow of the porch light, with his hands in his hoodie pockets. Head down. Lips moving.

I duck behind the gatepost, straining to hear.

He's on the phone—speaker mode.

"...I told you to keep your mouth shut," the voice says. Male. Gritty. "Don't bring up anything about Ring Zone tonight, you hear me? Not a damn word."

I freeze. My breath catches mid-chest.

Ring Zone.

Ian glances around, but not in the right direction. He doesn't see me. Doesn't know I'm here, tucked in the shadows like a ghost.

"My work is done," Ian mutters, his voice hushed but sharp. "Let Stanley chase his tail. He won't find it. Not unless someone runs their mouth."

He hangs up and shoves the phone deep into his jeans. Turns toward the house.

And that's when I step out from behind the cruiser.

"Ian."

He stops dead. Turns slowly. His face hardens the moment he sees me. Detective Stanley. Me.

"What the hell, Stanley? You following me now?"

"I need to know what you know about Ring Zone. Right now."

He looks over his shoulder like he's calculating how far he can run. I step in closer, low voice, firm but quiet.

"You were at the factory. You knew Raymond. You didn't just 'hear about the murder.' You're in it. And I'm done being polite."

He squares his jaw. "You got nothing on me."

"I got enough," I say, and pull a folded photo from my pocket. It's grainy, blown up from security footage.

"You recognize this man?" I ask.

Ian doesn't look. He stares at me.

And then—*crack.*

A branch snaps behind me. Loud. Too close.

I turn, instantly alert.

There's movement—just beyond the back fence. A silhouette, tall, watching. Then gone, vanished into the dark.

I spin back around.

Ian is gone.

Gone.

The photo flutters to the dirt.

I chase him around the house, pulse slamming in my ears.

But he's nowhere.

Then I hear the back gate creak.

And the faint sound of a second pair of footsteps—running.

Not Ian's.

Someone else.

Watching us both.

Chapter 18

bolt toward the back gate, my heart thundering like the bass still rattling the house behind me. The crowd has no idea what's unfolding just feet from their party—they're too busy dancing, drinking, pretending the world outside doesn't exist.

But I'm not pretending.

Not anymore.

The gate creaks again, slamming against the fence as I burst through it. I see shadows slicing through the alley. One is fast—lean, hunched, darting between garbage bins. Ian. Has to be.

But the other—

The other moves are different.

Calculated. Controlled. Like they've done this before.

I draw my weapon and sprint into the darkness, my shoes pounding the pavement, breath clouding in the night air. I round a corner and—

"Ian!" I yell.

No answer. Only footsteps, then silence.

Then I hear it.

A click.

Not a gun.

A phone.

Someone's recording me.

I whip around—no one.

Only the hum of a streetlight above, flickering like a pulse on its last breath.

I inch forward, back pressed to the brick wall. I holster my weapon, pull out my flashlight, and scan the alley.

Thereby, a dumpster.

A shoe. Just one. Black. Untied.

It's Ian's.

He left it behind.

I crouch to grab it when I hear the softest whisper, just feet from me.

A voice.

"You're getting close, detective."

I spin, light cutting through the dark.

But no one's there.

Just that voice, trailing off like smoke.

"You found Ian... now let's see if you can survive what comes next."

A door creaks open beside me. I don't hesitate—I kick it in.

And that's when I see it.

A wall covered in photos.

My face.

Raymond's.

Even Andre.

Red strings connect us all.

In the center—taped, torn, and stained with something that looks like blood—is Raymond's last security badge.

And beneath it.

A note.

Just four words, scrawled in shaky handwriting:

"You were too late."

Chapter 19

I sit in the back row of New Covenant Baptist, half-shaded by a wide pillar and a stack of abandoned Bibles. The air is thick—too many bodies packed into one building, not enough breeze to go around. Ceiling fans spin like they're exhausted, trying to beat back the heat and the spirit rising in the room.

It's Sunday morning, but this doesn't feel like any ordinary service. It feels like something's about to break.

Robert and his crew file in just before the final four seats vanish. All of them dressed up, caps still on, tassels dangling like medals of war. They look clean—sharpened up for the occasion. I wonder if any of them slept after the chaos at that party last night.

I didn't.

I'm not here to pray.

I'm here to watch.

"Can we say, 'Praise the Lord?'" the pastor shouts with a grin.

"Praise the Lord," the crowd thunders back.

I blend in, nodding, watching every movement. I'm two rows behind the graduates—just far enough that they don't notice me, just close enough that I can hear them whisper when the pastor calls them out.

"These fine young men," he says, "have endured much to get here. Let us give them a hand."

Applause erupts like a wave crashing against the stained-glass walls. But I'm watching Ian.

He's clapping like the rest, sure, but his eyes—his eyes scan the room like he's waiting on something. Or someone. They flick to the exit—the balcony. Then settle back on the pulpit.

Why so jumpy, Ian?

Ushers begin passing brass offering plates. Sabrina walks in right on cue, flanked by two of her friends. She's composed—like this is just another stop on her Sunday calendar. She drops a check into the plate, calm as ever.

Music swells. The choir begins another number. A woman faints from the spirit. People shout, run, and wave fans like swords.

But I don't move.

Deadly Oath

Liz is singing now—*Give, and I Give It Back to You*—and while the others are catching the Holy Ghost, I'm catching every eye twitch and nervous glance in the pews ahead of me.

Service draws to a close—or so I think—until the pastor grabs the mic again.

"Sabrina, will you please come forward?"

A ripple moves through the crowd. Even Robert shifts in his seat.

Sabrina doesn't flinch. She walks down the aisle like she knew this was coming.

"Lead us in the next hymn," the pastor says, handing her the mic.

Her voice rises above the music. It's strong. Too strong for someone who's just supposed to be a guest. The choir backs her up, tambourines shaking like warning bells.

"You should be a witness," she sings, eyes closed.

But I'm not looking at her anymore.

I'm looking at Ian.

He's leaning toward Robert now, whispering something in his ear. Robert nods once—barely—but then he glances back, right over his shoulder.

Right at me.

And freezes.

Our eyes lock.

He elbows Ian.

Ian turns. His face drains of color.

They weren't expecting me.

Robert mouths something I can't hear over the music, but I read the shape of the words.

"We have to go."

I rise from my seat.

And just then—

A phone buzzes in Ian's lap.

He answers it without hesitation, sliding it under his jacket.

All I hear is one word before he bolts up from the pew.

"Now."

I push through the crowd, but I'm too late. The four men are already sliding past stunned ushers and slipping through the side door into the parking lot.

Sabrina keeps singing like nothing happened.

"You should be a witness for Jesus..."

But I'm not chasing salvation today.

I'm chasing the truth.

The suspects have just left the building.

Chapter 20

'm still reeling from what I overheard last night—
Ian on that call, speaking the words *Ring Zone* like
it was just another errand. The man tried to play it
cool, but something was off, and I wasn't letting go of it.

Sunday evening settles like a heavy coat. The warmth
of the church has worn off, and I'm back at my desk,
combing through files, when an alert pings my phone. It's
an email from a name I almost forgot. **Lexi.**

The subject line: "Thought You Should See This."

I click. Inside is a photo attachment and a short
message:

*I took this photo of Raymond a week before he died.
He didn't know someone was watching him. Look closely in
the reflection.*

I open the image.

It's a grainy shot—Raymond stands outside of Ring Zone near the dumpster, mid-conversation with a man who has mostly turned his face away. Nothing unusual at first glance—until I zoom in.

There, in the window's reflection behind them, is a figure. Partially hidden. But the outline is unmistakable. Tall. Stocky. Wearing a jacket with the Caught Security logo.

I freeze the frame and run it through the enhancement software on my laptop. I sharpen the shadows.

A name punches into my brain like a sledgehammer.

Robert.

My breathing slows. That's the same night he said he was with Lexi.

I check the time stamp—11:48 p.m.

Raymond's estimated time of death? Between 11:30 and 12:00.

My phone buzzes again.

Another message. This one is from Andre.

"Call me. We got movement. One of the guards—Shawn—just turned up in police custody during a traffic stop. He asked for you. Said it's about Ring Zone."

My heart's hammering now.

Deadly Oath

I grab my keys, holster my badge, and bolt out of the precinct. This night just cracked wide open.

And if Shawn is ready to talk

Someone's secrets are about to bleed.

Chapter 21

The holding room reeks of stale sweat and fear. Fluorescent lights hum above me like a warning, the kind you get right before the truth explodes in your face. Shawn sits across the metal table—hands folded, leg bouncing, his eyes refusing to meet mine.

I lean forward slowly, arms crossed.

"Start talking."

He swallows hard. "You came. I didn't think you would."

I don't blink. "You said it's about Ring Zone. You've got one shot, Shawn. Don't waste it."

He exhales. Long. Shaky. Then, finally meets my eyes.

"I was on shift the week before Raymond died. Midnight rotation. That place was off, like someone was watching us, but not on the cameras. Like someone else was watching the watchers."

"Who?"

He rubs his face. "There was a guy. He wasn't assigned there. Said he was temp. Floated between sites. Real quiet, real smooth. The name was Ian. Came in with a badge, but something about it was off. Too clean. Never signed the logbook. The security manager cleared Ian to work, but no one ever vetted him. My stomach flips.

"Ian?"

"Yeah. The same Ian who was at that party last night. Same Ian, I saw you standing outside the break room with Raymond the night before it happened. They were arguing."

"What were they arguing about?"

"I don't know. But I caught one line. Raymond said, 'You think I'm gonna let this slide just because of who you know?' And Ian—he just smiled and said, 'I don't think you understand how deep this goes.'"

I grip the edge of the table.

That's not just a dispute. That's a warning.

I stand up. "You've just changed everything."

Shawn's voice cracks as I reach the door. "Am I in danger, Detective?"

I turn, lock eyes with him.

"If you're telling the truth... you've been in danger this whole time."

I step into the hallway, pulse hammering. Everything is connecting. The party. The call. The photo. The argument.

Ian's not just involved.

He's connected to someone bigger.

I fish my phone from my coat, ready to call Andre—

And that's when it vibrates.

No name.

Just a message.

Stop digging, Stanley. Or you're next.

I look up.

The hallway is empty.

Or so I thought.

From the end of the corridor, a shadow moves.

Chapter 22

'm back at the precinct now, standing in front of the evidence board, arms crossed, eyes narrowed. The lights are low, the station half-empty, but my brain's on fire.

Too many pieces.

Too many players.

I don't even hear Andre come in until he clears his throat behind me.

"You're burning a hole in that board, Stanley," he says, setting a paper cup of coffee on my desk. "Might want to drink something before your head explodes."

I don't look away from the board. Not yet.

"You ever feel like a case is talking to you, Andre? Like the answers are right there, just buried under bullshit?"

"Every damn time," he mutters, pulling a chair beside mine. "Walk me through it again."

I nod toward the wall.

"Start with Dominic. He says he only worked at Ring Zone for a week, then he was transferred to a new location. Claims he never met Raymond. Says Shawn trained him."

"And you believe that?" Andre asks.

"I believe... he's scared. I watched his body language. He's holding something back. But the thing is, he mentioned Shawn too easily. Like he *wanted* to point me there."

Andre squints. "So Dominic could be deflecting?"

"Or he's baiting me," I say. "Shawn's name keeps popping up. He trained Raymond. He's connected to Ian, Robert, and even Wyatt—they all hang out at school, at parties, and they talk. But they're always a little too rehearsed."

Andre crosses his arms. "And Shawn? What did he say when you spoke to him?"

I turn slowly to face him now. "He said he trained Raymond. Said he's never seen anything suspicious—until now. Said he's scared. But it was the way he said it. Not scared of what happened. Scared of what *someone might say.*"

Andre leans forward, lowering his voice. "Which one of them do you think snapped, John?"

I look back at the board. Harsh fluorescent lighting clips each photo..

Dominic. Robert. Ian. Shawn. Wyatt`.

"They're all covering for each other," I mutter. "But the weakest link's cracking. I heard Ian on the phone—he told someone to shut up about Ring Zone. Then ran his mouth just long enough to make me think *he's* not the killer."

Andre runs a hand over his face. "And what about Robert?"

I tighten my jaw.

"Robert's got a temper. We've seen that. But it's more than that—he's the *center.* These guys orbit around him. He's the one who always has to keep things calm until someone pokes him. And when I shook his hand the other night, he flinched."

Andre raises a brow. "Flinched?"

"His knuckles were raw, healing," I say. "You don't get that from bartending."

We fall into silence.

The board stares back at us.

"So what's the next move?" Andre finally asks.

I step closer to the board and tap Raymond's photo. "We're missing a thread. Something small. Something they all know—but no one's saying."

A phone buzzes.

Mine.

I check the screen.

Blocked number.

I answer anyway. "Stanley."

There's static. Then a voice.

"She knows," it whispers. Female. Unsteady. "She's gonna tell you. She said she couldn't keep it to herself anymore. Meet her at the park. Tonight. By the swing set."

"Who is this? Who's gonna talk?" I press.

The voice trembles.

"She saw what they did after the party. She was there. She saw *everything*."

Click.

The line goes dead.

Andre watches me closely. "Who was that?"

I grab my coat. "I don't know. But if what the voice says is true, one of those boys didn't just kill Raymond; they *planned it*. Together."

Outside, thunder rolls low in the distance.

The swing set waits.

And someone's about to break.

Chapter 23

The park is almost empty when I pull up. It's past 11. The wind cuts through the trees, rustling the leaves in restless whispers. Streetlamps cast yellow pools of light, but everything between them feels like shadows and secrets.

I step out of the car and scan the grounds. My hand rests on my holster, out of habit.

A rusty swing creaks.

There. By the swing set—someone's sitting, hunched forward, legs tucked up like they're trying to fold into themselves.

I approach slowly, boots crunching across the gravel.

She lifts her head. It's Lexi.

My gut twists.

"You called me?" I ask, keeping my voice low.

She nods but doesn't speak.

"I need to know what you saw," I say. "Tonight. Now. Before someone else gets hurt."

She looks around like she expects shadows to lunge from the trees.

"I didn't call you," she whispers. "But she did."

"She?"

Lexi reaches into her purse and pulls out a burner phone. And thrust it into my hand as if it's searing her skin.

She was at the party. She stayed late. She said she saw something in the alley behind Robert's house. The guys— Dominic, Ian, Shawn, Wyatt, and Robert."

She takes a shaky breath.

"The men were arguing. Loud. And then someone said, 'We buried him too deep for them to find anything.'"

I go cold.

"She ran. Didn't want to get involved. But tonight she cracked. She told me that she saw what they were carrying. A duffel bag. Heavy."

I kneel in front of her. "Where is she now?"

Lexi's eyes fill with panic.

"She was supposed to meet me here. But she's not answering anymore."

Deadly Oath

Just then, the burner phone in my hand lights up.

Unknown Number.

I answer. "This is Detective Stanley."

Heavy breathing. Then a whisper.

"They know I talked. Someone followed me. I think—I think they're going to—"

The line goes dead.

I bolt to my feet, scanning the tree line. A movement—a shape—slips between the trees behind the tennis courts. My heart pounds like thunder in my ears.

"Lexi, get back in your car. Lock the doors. Now."

I draw my weapon and move toward the shadows.

Whoever's out there is running now.

But they made one mistake.

They came back to clean up the mess.

And I'm right on their trail.

Chapter 24

I move through the trees, weapon drawn, every nerve on fire. The flashlight beam cuts through branches. I hear something—quick footsteps, heavy breathing, snapping twigs. Whoever I'm chasing isn't being careful. They're running scared.

I catch a glimpse of the figure, wearing a dark hoodie and cap pulled low, moving quickly. But the person isn't as fast as they think. "Stop!" I shout.

No response. Just the crunch of shoes tearing through dirt and brush. I push harder, faster, vaulting over a fallen log. There's a clearing up ahead. A small maintenance shack. And then silence.

I slow down.

Too quiet.

I circle wide, flashlight off now, letting my eyes adjust.

The shack door swings, creaking just slightly.

They're inside.

I edge forward, back against the outer wall. I count to three. Kick the door open.

Empty.

Except for the smell—burnt rubber. And smoke.

There's a scorched phone on the ground. Still warm. Someone torched it seconds before I got here.

But something's under it.

A photo.

Raymond and Ian. Arms around each other. Matching security jackets.

Brothers in uniform.

So why did Ian lie and say he barely knew him?

Before I can think, my phone buzzes. It's Andre.

"John, where the hell are you?"

"While tracking the person who torched the phone, I found something they left behind—evidence that Raymond and Ian were closer than we thought."

"You're not gonna believe this," Andre says, voice tight. "We ran background checks deeper on your suspects."

"Yeah?"

"Dominic, Robert, Wyatt, Shawn—they've all been linked to the *same* off-the-books security detail three years ago. The same firm that disbanded after a theft case went cold. Guess who handled payroll?"

I already know the answer.

"Ian."

"Bingo. And it gets worse. That burner Lexi handed you? The phone pinged off a tower one block from your station."

I freeze.

"I'm coming in now."

"No," Andre says. "Don't. That call didn't come from the city."

I stare at the phone in my hand.

"Then where?"

Andre doesn't speak for a moment.

Then: "It came from Raymond Stanley's old number-- The one that was disconnected after he died."

My blood runs cold.

"Impossible."

"You tell me, partner."

I stare at the photo. Raymond and Ian are both smiling.

But someone else is in the background. Just barely visible.

A shadow between them.

Someone I recognize.

But it's not possible.

Unless.

I zoom in.

And I see him.

Chapter 25

ndre leans against my desk, arms folded, face hard as concrete. He's been quiet for too long, and that means he's about to say something that'll knock the air out of my lungs.

I toss the file on the table between us—Dominic West's employment history. He was only at Ring Zone for a week, but that's a week too long for someone who "barely remembers the place." My gut's not buying his innocence, no matter how many times he throws his hands up and swears he's clean.

"You got anything new?" I ask.

Andre nods, flipping through his phone. "Yeah. I ran traces of the social connections between our suspects—

Dominic, Robert, Ian, Shawn, and Wyatt. They're all tied tighter than a noose."

He tosses me a photo. It's an old one—a party. Dim lights and red cups, but the faces are clear. All five suspects—together. Arms around each other. Laughing.

"You see that?" he says, pointing to the corner.

I lean closer. My chest tightens.

Lexi.

She's off to the side, not smiling. Not part of the hug-fest. But she's there. Watching. Listening.

"She's the thread," I mutter. "She's been close to all of them. She was the one who mentioned Dominic first, remember? And she gave me that album with Shawn in it."Andre nods slowly. "And yet, every time she talks, it's like she's leaving something out."

"Too careful," I say.

"Too controlled," he adds.

We sit in silence for a moment. Then I say what we're both thinking.

"She might not just be a witness."

Andre raises an eyebrow. "She might be protecting someone."

I stand up and pace the room. The pieces are starting to align, but they're jagged. Dangerous.

"Let's run through this," I say. "Dominic claims the company transferred to another site," Ian said. He didn't know Raymond, but there was a photo of the two of them in matching uniforms. Robert's temper flares faster than a matchstick. Wyatt plays the background. But I watched him at that party. He doesn't miss a damn thing. And Shawn? He trained Raymond. And now he's acting like he barely remembers him."

Andre leans forward. "They're circling the truth. Protecting each other. Or protecting something."

I nod. "Maybe someone."

There's a knock at the door.

A rookie pokes his head in. "Detective Stanley? You might want to come down to evidence."

"What is it?"

"We pulled the hard drive off a security terminal at Ring Zone. Someone wiped it. But our tech just recovered partial footage."

Andre and I lock eyes.

"We're coming."

As we head for the stairs, I stop short.

"Andre," I whisper.

"Yeah?"

"If Lexi's been close to them this whole time... what if she saw something that night?"

Andre doesn't answer right away.

Then: "Or worse. What if Lexi helped cover it up?"

My blood runs cold.

Downstairs, the tech is waiting, already cueing up the recovered footage.

The screen flickers. A loading bar crawls forward.

Then the image stabilizes.

And what we see makes my throat tighten.

It's footage from two nights before the murder.

Raymond's sitting in the guard station.

Talking to someone off-camera.

The voice is muffled but familiar.

And then, she steps into frame.

Lexi.

Chapter 26

The room is dead silent. Just the soft hum of the monitor and my heartbeat rattling in my ears.

Lexi.

She's standing right there, clear as day, on the screen in front of me—inside the guard booth at Ring Zone—two nights before Raymond's murder.

She leans in close to him. She's smiling, but it doesn't feel warm. It feels *intentional*. Calculated.

"What the hell…" I murmur.

Andre is already pacing.

"She said she hadn't been to that site in months," he mutters, his jaw tight.

"She lied."

The video's timestamp flickers. 11:12 p.m. The camera angle is tight, but I can see Raymond hand her something—a folder or envelope, maybe. She tucks it into her purse, just like Lexi has done a hundred times.

Then, as she turns to leave, Raymond glances over his shoulder, uneasy. Like he's being watched.

The footage ends in static.

"Playback ends there," the tech says. "The rest is corrupted."

"Of course it is," Andre spits.

I stare at the frozen screen. That moment—Raymond watching the door—something about it sticks with me. There's fear in his face. As if he knew that moment would be one of his last.

"She's hiding something," I say aloud.

"No doubt. And you can't ignore who Lexi is connected to." Andre crosses his arms. "Robert. Ian. Shawn. Dominic. Wyatt. All of them. She's like the common denominator in a toxic equation."

I grab my coat. "We need to talk to her. Now."

We head out the back door of the station, avoiding the front desk and the press that lurk by the windows. I slide into the cruiser, fire up the engine, and take the long way around the block. Just in case someone's watching. Something tells me they are.

"Where is she now?" Andre asks as he pulls out his phone.

"The last address she gave us was off West Chicago Avenue. I'll call dispatch."

But before I can even hit dial, my phone buzzes.

Unknown Number.

I hesitate to answer.

"Detective Stanley," I say.

There's a pause. Then a voice.

"Stop looking for Lexi."

My stomach tightens.

"Who is this?"

The line clicks dead.

I pull the car over hard, tires screeching. Andre is already on edge, gripping the handle of his door.

"You heard that?"

He nods. "We're getting too close."

I shift into drive again.

And just as I turn the corner onto her block, I see the door to Lexi's building wide open.

The glass is shattered.

A trail of blood leads down the stairs.

Deadly Oath

I throw the car in park and step out with my hand on my weapon, and Andre is right behind me.

We enter slow. Careful.

The building smells like copper and panic.

"Lexi?" I call out.

No answer.

Then I hear it.

A soft, metallic click from the stairwell below.

Someone's still here.

And they're not alone.

Chapter 27

t's a little after eleven when I park two blocks from the club. I kill the engine and let the silence settle over me. The night air is thick, hanging like a shroud over this part of town. Most of the bar crowd has already spilled out, laughing and drunk, looking for cars, rides, or trouble.

But I'm not watching them.

I'm watching her.

Angela.

She walks out of the bar with her arms folded tightly, her black dress catching the wind like it's trying to whisper a warning. She doesn't know I'm here. She thinks she's alone. But I need to be sure. Ever since Raymond's murder, I've been tracking threads, and one of them leads to her.

She's heading to her car, parked three blocks down on a dimly lit side street. I keep my distance, walking the sidewalk across from hers. Her purse swings as she fumbles in it, finally fishing out her keys. I slow near a parked van and pause, shielded in shadow.

She freezes.

A noise—too close behind her.

She spins, keys clenched in her fist, but sees no one. Then she darts inside the car, slams the door shut, and locks it. I feel the urge to step in, but I stop myself. She hasn't seen him yet. I haven't seen him yet. But I can feel it.

Something is wrong.

Then her window rolls down a crack, and a man whistles from a passing car.

"Hey, baby, can I go?"

She smiles—tight-lipped, polite. Just enough to avoid trouble. Another man in a black Mustang creeps past slower, waiting for a response that never comes.

"Bitch!" he yells, tires screeching as he peels off, smoke curling into the air like a warning flare.

Angela exhales hard. I see her glance at her phone, then answer it.

I move closer, careful not to be seen. I can hear Angela now—bits and pieces of her conversation with her sister.

"I just needed space... I wanted to go out and have a drink."

"You went alone?" her sister asks, clearly not happy.

Angela laughs. "I'm fine. I'm going home now."

She hangs up, tosses her phone into the passenger seat, and starts singing along to the radio—Mary J. Blige. Something about the way she sings makes the scene feel normal.

Safe.

But I know better.

Then she jolts. A rustle—paper, maybe. Something is shifting in the backseat?

Her head snaps to the side mirror. I see her eyes scan the alley.

The wind kicks up. Lights in the surrounding shops flicker and die. The street seems to go darker. Tighter. I instinctively reach for my sidearm.

Then—movement.

A woman with blonde hair and dark sunglasses walks by slowly. Too slow. Angela watches her too. So do I. But the woman turns the corner and disappears.

Angela drops the car into reverse.

But before she can pull away, she screams.

Loud. Piercing. Ripping through the night.

I sprint across the street.

But I'm too far away to stop it.

Through the windshield, I see the shape in the backseat—*him*.

Sam.

His hand yanks her hair back viciously. The blade flashes once before plunging deep into her neck. I shout— "ANGELA!"—but my voice is drowned by the sound of her horn. She thrashes once, then goes limp over the wheel. Blood streaks the windshield in a fan of red.

Sam opens the door and slips out—face obscured, calm as a shadow—and vanishes into the alley.

Click-clack. Click-clack. The sound of his boots echoes as he fades into darkness.

I reach her car seconds too late. My hands are trembling.

But that's not the worst part.

As I look at Angela's lifeless body, slumped forward, I see it—a note pinned to her shoulder with the blade still lodged in her skin.

Three words, scrawled in red ink:

"You were warned."

Chapter 28

R ed and blue lights slice through the dark as Andre pulls up to the scene. Sirens wail in the distance—backups closing in. He throws the car into park and steps into the chaos. Flashing lights, yellow tape, a crowd pressing too close, trying to get a glimpse of the horror they'll never unsee.

"All right, everyone—stand back!" I shout, lifting the tape and ducking underneath. My badge flashes as I march toward the cluster of uniforms near the vehicle. The coroner's van is already here, doors open, gurney waiting.

Andre turns when he sees me, jaw clenched, his face paler than usual.

"Another woman?" he asks.

I nod, grim. "Same pattern. Stab wound to the neck—but this time the woman's neck is snapped clean. She didn't even get the chance to scream."

I step toward the car, and the smell of copper thickens in the air. Her head is slumped over the steering wheel, face hidden in her blood. I reach in and gently push her back against the seat, and Andre's stomach drops.

Angela.

The woman from the last scene. The one who had answers in her eyes but stayed guarded.

"Damn it," he mutters.

"You remember her?" I ask.

He nods slowly. "She was scared then. Guess she had reason to be."

We start canvassing the area, flashlights sweeping across the pavement, up the walls, under the car. Then, I feel something nudge against my boot. I stop. Shine my light down.

Something dark. Something small.

I kneel, reach for it.

A knife.

Black handle. Dried blood crusted along the edge.

"Andre!" I call out, holding it up.

He's beside me in seconds. "Son of a—he left it?"

"No," I say, my voice low. "He *wanted* us to find it."

We bag it, tag it. I radio dispatch. "This is Detective Stanley. We need a sweep of the entire area. Five-block radius. K9 support. He's not far."

Andre turns in a slow circle, scanning rooftops, alleys, and fire escapes. The hairs on the back of my neck are standing.

I start questioning people in the crowd—nothing. No one saw a thing. Or at least they're too scared to say they did.

But then I feel it. That sense.

That someone's watching.

Across the street, a figure stands half-swallowed by shadows. I can't make out the face, but I know. My instincts know.

Sam.

He doesn't move. Doesn't flinch. Just watches.

Then slowly, he smiles.

And vanishes into the alley.

"Andre!" I shout. "He's here! HE'S HERE!"

We take off running.

But he's already gone.

And I know now.

The murders won't stop.

Not until one of us is dead.

Chapter 29

I head back to the precinct, gripping the steering wheel tighter than usual. Angela's murder has me twisted up inside. It's not just another case—it's a message. Andre is already waiting in the bullpen when I step in, leaning over a stack of reports.

"Man, what do you think?" I ask, tossing my keys on the desk.

"About what?" he says without looking up.

"The case," I reply, sharper than I mean to. My head's buzzing, the pieces don't fit—yet.

Before Andre can answer, Sergeant Carl Smith strolls over like he's got nothing but time. His walk is slow, too casual. He's holding something behind his back.

"You boys talking about the girl who got sliced up in her home?" he says with a grin that makes my skin crawl.

"Yeah. You got something to add?" I ask, cautiously.

Carl lifts his right hand—a knife. Long, gleaming, wicked-looking. In his other hand? A rag doll—stuffed, worn, with a red hat and candy-striped blouse. He lifts the doll, then slams the blade into its soft gut.

"If I'd done it," he sneers, twisting the knife in a sickening circle, "I'd cut her from neck to navel... and watch the floor drink every drop."

Sand from the doll spills onto the precinct tiles like blood.

"You're sick," Andre mutters.

Carl laughs. "You gotta think like a killer to catch one."

The way his voice echoes—mocking, hollow—it stays with me as Sergeant Jenkins yells from his office.

"John! Andre! In here. Now!"

We rush inside.

He slams three files down in front of us. "Three dead women. Same method. Two at the same address—Fatima upstairs, Angela downstairs. The third, Cindy, was across town."

My throat tightens. "So we've got a serial?"

Jenkins nods. "But it's messy. Two were Black, one white. All corporate. No clear motive. I want to know what connects them. Give me something."

"We've got similarities," I say, flipping through the photos, "but no forensics, no witnesses."

"Then we start looking deeper," Jenkins snaps. "Passion, revenge, random thrill? Hell, I don't care what kind of demented person this is. I want a name."

Andre leans forward. "Any chance it's Ryan Hill?"

I freeze. Ryan Hill. The monster from the '90s. Six women. All slaughtered in their beds.

"He's out," Jenkins says, lighting a cigarette with hands that don't shake nearly enough. "Released two days ago. DNA cleared him after decades. Now he's staying in a halfway house—near the damn crime scenes."

Andre and I exchange a look. No way that's a coincidence.

We head out with a warrant. And sure enough, the halfway house is a stone's throw from where Angela and Fatima's bodies were found. We stake it out from an unmarked cruiser.

People pass by. A candy-apple-red Corvette pulls up, and a buff guy hops out. Mrs. James is watering her lawn across the street. She spots us.

"You boys find anything?" she whispers when we cross over. "I heard stories. Some folks say it was a man. Others say a woman."

She leans in closer. "Or maybe... both."

I nod, not sure what to say. Mrs. James' words hang in the air like fog.

Inside Angela's house, crime scene tape still flutters at the edges. Degrees on the walls. Family photos. Everything feels too normal for somewhere soaked in death. Forensics already cleared it, but we check again.

Upstairs at Fatima's, the place is chaos: broken glass, overturned chairs, papers scattered like confetti after a massacre.

Then Andre stops.

"John. Look at this."

He hands me a torn piece of paper: *1815... 25.* On the floor nearby—old lottery tickets. I flip the paper over. Blank.

"This means anything to you?"

"No idea," I mutter. But it feels like something.

Back downstairs, we scan Angela's photos. One picture grabs me. She's on the lap of a man with a city employee uniform—the name on his chest: *Nathaniel.*

"Looks like we've got a boyfriend," I say, bagging the photo.

Andre finds a similar picture in Fatima's place. Another guy. Uniform. Name: *Aaron.*

We're back at the station in minutes. Phone records just came in. Fatima's most frequent caller? Angela. Second most? Aaron.

Angela's? Nathaniel.

Andre dials Aaron first.

"Detroit PD. We need to ask you a few questions."

"What's this about?" Aaron barks.

"We just need—"

"I didn't kill anybody," he snaps. "Talk to my lawyer."
Click.

I call Nathaniel.

"This is Detective Stanley—"

"Don't put me in that mess with Angela," he snaps.
Click.

The next day, both of them show up—lawyers in tow.

We split up. I take Aaron.

"You know her?" I say, sliding Fatima's photo across the table.

He smirks. "Yeah. We dated."

"You ever hit her?"

"I may have. Gotta keep her in line."

I lean in close. "I'll prove what you did. And when I do, I'll bury you."

He laughs as officers escort him out.

In the other room, Andre works with Nathaniel.

By the time we reconvene, my head's pounding.

"This thing's escalating," I mutter.

Then one of the rookies pokes his head in. "Hey... someone just left this on your desk."

It's a red envelope.

No name. No return address.

I tear it open.

Inside a photo.

Angela. Taken from behind. Walking alone at night.

And scrawled across the bottom in red ink:

"NEXT, I COME FOR YOU."

I glance at Andre. His eyes narrow. My mouth goes dry.

Because on the back of the photo.is the same number from the paper in Fatima's house:

1815... 25.

Chapter 30

t's just after 10:30 p.m. when I kill the headlights and ease my unmarked car into a shadowed corner across from Sabrina's apartment complex. I've been watching this place for two nights straight, and something tells me tonight will break open more than one layer of this case. The air is thick with tension—or maybe that's just me, wired on caffeine and instinct.

That's when I see them.

Shawn and Sabrina. They're leaning against a midnight-blue sedan parked just feet from her front door. Her red dress flutters slightly in the breeze, the moonlight catching her profile just enough for me to make out the concern etched into her face. Shawn leans in close. Their voices are low, but the night's quiet, and I crack the window just enough to hear.

"I'm serious, Sabrina," Shawn says, glancing nervously over his shoulder. "You should've told me the moment you saw him."

"I didn't want to ruin the night," she replies, folding her arms across her chest. "Besides, I only caught a glimpse of him at the restaurant. Could've been anyone."

"No," Shawn says. His tone hardens. "You said you saw someone near your apartment last night, too. Same guy?"

"I think so," she admits. "Same height. Same build. But the man kept his head low. I never got a clear look."

I shift in my seat. My gut coils tight. Someone's following Sabrina—and it's not just me. But this guy, whoever he is, doesn't want her watched. He wants her scared. He wants control.

Sabrina continues, softer now. "He was standing by that tree across from the valet stand, just watching. No phone. No reason to be there."

Shawn curses under his breath. "He could've followed us. Back here. Right now."

I lean closer, every muscle in my body wound tight like piano wire. Something's coming. I feel it in the pit of my stomach, crawling up my spine like a warning.

"You think he's the one?" Sabrina whispers. "The one from the news?"

"I don't know," Shawn replies, barely audible. "But those women... Angela, Fatima, and Cindy all worked in the HR department. You did too. Remember?"

Her breath catches. "That was months ago, Shawn. I barely even knew them."

"But your name could've been on one of those resumes," he mutters.

That's when I see it. Movement. A silhouette shifting behind the complex. Near the alley. Slow. Deliberate.

Not me.

I reach for my radio. "This is Detective Stanley," I whisper into the mic. "Surveillance on Sabrina Kelley's residence. We've got a potential hostile nearby. Request immediate backup. Quiet approach. Repeat—quiet."

I keep my eyes locked on the figure creeping just outside the glow of the streetlamp. He's not moving toward them. Not yet. He's watching, same as me. But the difference is—I've got a badge. He's got a plan.

"I'm walking you up," Shawn says to Sabrina. "I don't care what you say."

They start toward her door, unaware of what is happening. The shadow behind the building slinks closer, pressing tight against the wall, waiting for the right moment.

I step out of the car, gun holstered but ready, and keep to the darkness, staying close to the edge of the lot. One wrong move, one wrong sound, and this night goes sideways.

Sabrina laughs lightly, trying to shake off the dread. "You're being paranoid, Shawn."

"No," I whisper to myself, watching the shadow step forward, inches from the blind spot between the stairwell and the dumpster. "You're being hunted."

And then—

A scream rips through the air.

Not Sabrina. Not Shawn.

It comes from deeper in the alley.

I draw my weapon. Backup's not here yet. My feet move before my brain can catch up, gun raised, badge flashing in the dark.

"Police! Show me your hands!"

But no one answers.

And that's when I see the message.

Etched in chalk on the wall near the dumpster.

"I'm watching. She's next."

Chapter 31

My flashlight cuts through the darkness like a blade. The message glows faintly under the beam—just enough for me to taste the malice behind it.

I'm watching. She's next.

"Son of a—" I exhale through clenched teeth, sweeping the alley for movement. Nothing. Whoever was here is already gone—ghost steps. Clean exit.

I press my radio. "Stanley to Dispatch. I've got a threat left at the scene—alley wall behind Sabrina Kelley's apartment. The suspect fled on foot. I need CSU and backup here five minutes ago."

"Copy that, Detective Stanley. Units en route."

I lower the radio and freeze. Footsteps. Close. Not running. Walking.

Back toward Sabrina's door.

I grip my weapon and round the corner, fast and low. My heart hammers like a war drum. But it's only Shawn. He's standing there alone in front of the apartment, knocking.

"Sabrina?" he calls, knocking again. "Hey... open up."

The lights are still on inside. But no answer.

I holster my gun and step out of the shadows.

"Shawn," I say sharply.

He jolts, spinning around. "Jesus, man! You scared me."

"What are you doing out here?"

"Sabrina ran back in to grab her phone. She never came back out."

I look up at the second-floor window. The light flickers once, then goes out.

Something's wrong.

I rush past him and draw my weapon again. "Stay here."

"Wait—what's going on?" he asks, stepping toward me.

I stop him cold with one look. "Now, Shawn. Stay."

Deadly Oath

I kick open the front door. It bangs against the wall as I sweep inside, clearing each corner. The apartment is dead silent. The air smells like perfume and something else. Something sharp.

Upstairs.

I take the stairs two at a time.

"Sabrina?" I call out.

No answer.

Her bedroom door is slightly ajar, light bleeding out from beneath. I push it open—

Empty.

But the window is open. Curtains fluttering in the wind.

Then I see it—her phone on the bed, screen shattered—a smear of something dark along the edge of the frame.

"Sabrina..." I whisper.

Suddenly—

The closet door creaks.

I whip around, gun raised.

But it's not what I expect.

It's empty.

Just a note. Taped inside.

I step closer, heart jackhammering.

In thick red marker, block letters read:

"You're too late. Tick tock, detective."

My radio crackles. Backups's arriving.

Too late.

Sabrina is gone.

Chapter 32

Red and blue lights strobe through the window. I bolt downstairs just as the first unit screeches to a stop outside. Officers fan out, weapons drawn, scanning the perimeter. I motion them inside.

"She's gone!" I bark. "The suspect got in and out clean—left a message upstairs. I need eyes on every alley, every exit, every rooftop."

The first officer nods and runs out with a flashlight.

Andre barrels through the door a second later, panting hard. "What the hell happened?"

"The killer was here," I snap, pulling him toward the stairs. "He took Sabrina. Left a damn note in her closet."

"Jesus Christ..."

We reach the bedroom, and I point at the open window. The curtains are still swaying. The note is still there, taped to the closet wall like a trophy.

Andre reads it out loud. "You're too late. Tick tock, detective."

He looks at me. "Tick tock? What the hell does that mean?"

I grit my teeth. "It means we're on a clock now."

He glances down at the smear of blood on the phone. "You think Sabrina's still alive?"

"She better be," I mutter. "Or this whole city's about to burn."

My radio crackles again. "Detective Stanley, this is Officer Reed. We've got a neighbor claiming they saw a figure in a hoodie jump from the second-floor balcony onto the fire escape. Headed west down the alley."

"Keep following. Don't engage. Just keep eyes glued."

I spin on my heel and head out the door, Andre right behind me.

As we get into the car, something in the pit of my stomach twists.

Because I've seen this pattern before—each murder more calculated, more brazen.

And this time, it's personal.

The killer's watching us, taunting me.

And Sabrina is the bait.

I throw the car into gear.

"Where are we going?" Andre asks, gripping the dashboard.

"To find someone who can help us understand what 'tick tock' really means."

He frowns. "Who?"

I stare into the darkness ahead.

"Dominic."

He stiffens. "Sabrina's brother?"

I nod slowly. "Yeah. And the last man who had a key to this apartment."

Chapter 33

I'm already out of the car before it entirely stops, charging toward Robert's building. Uniforms are fanned out across the lot, shouting to one another, flashlights sweeping shadows like swords.

I take the stairs two at a time. Third floor. End unit. The door swings open before I knock.

Robert stands there, shirt half-buttoned, wide-eyed, phone still clutched in his hand.

"John..." he breathes. "You—you heard what happened, right?"

"I was the one chasing the car that shot your neighbor," I say, brushing past him into the apartment. "Tell me everything. Now."

He closes the door and follows me inside, still shaken. "I was in here. My neighbor, Elijah, is outside smoking. I was on the phone with a man about a job interview at an insurance company, a legitimate opportunity. Then I heard it pop, fast ones. Gunshots."

"You see who fired?"

He shakes his head. "No. By the time I got outside, Elijah was screaming, bleeding all over the concrete. His sock was soaked."

I nod toward the kitchen table, where a notepad sits. Scribbled on it in sloppy ink: *Tuesday. 10 AM. Interview.*

"You still planning to go?"

Robert looks at me like I'm crazy. "That was before. Now I don't even know if I should leave the damn apartment."

"That interview may be your only normal thing left," I say. "Don't skip it."

He stares at me, then quietly nods.

I take a slow breath and lean against the wall. "Let's talk about the party. The night Cindy was murdered."

He flinches at her name.

"I didn't do anything," he says fast. "I wasn't even near that woman."

"That's not what I asked."

He hesitates.

"I saw her," he admits. "I saw all of them. Angela, Fatima, and Cindy. They were laughing at guys like me.

Like we didn't even exist, they turned down everyone at the job fair. Like they were gods."

"That bother you?"

"Wouldn't it bother you?" he snaps, then quickly reins it in. "I mean… it was frustrating. But that doesn't mean I killed anybody."

I nod slowly, eyes scanning the apartment. The same scent lingers from earlier—smoke, sweat, and something else, metallic.

Then I see it.

On the floor, just barely sticking out from under the recliner. A cufflink. Polished. Out of place. I kneel and pick it up.

"Yours?" I ask, holding it up.

Robert squints at it. "Nah. That ain't mine."

Andre's voice crackles in my earpiece. *"John, where are you?"*

"Inside with Robert," I answer. "Find anything at Sabrina's?"

"Blood on the phone. No sign of her. Killer left a message: 'You're too late. Tick tock.'"

I freeze. "Say that again."

"Tick tock, detective. That's what it said."

My stomach knots. I glance at Robert. "Have you ever heard that phrase before? Tick tock?"

He looks confused. "No… why?"

"Because it's not just a message," I mutter. "It's a timeline. A countdown."

"To what?" Andre asks.

I don't answer.

Because I already know.

It's happening again.

I pocket the cufflink and walk to the window. Across the street, under the glow of a broken streetlamp, a black Honda idles. Engine running. No plates.

I narrow my eyes.

That's no coincidence.

"Stay inside," I tell Robert. "And don't open that door for anyone. You understand?"

He nods, but something in his face tells me he's hiding more. I don't press—not yet. There's a knock at the door.

Once. Then twice. Slow. Deliberate.

Robert freezes. "You expecting someone?"

"No," I whisper, drawing my weapon.

I approach the door and peer through the peephole.

No one there.

Then I hear it—a soft *click* from the back window.

The same one facing the fire escape.

I turn back to Robert, my voice a low growl.

"Stay behind me."

I move to the hallway, every sense sharp.

Because if I'm right, the killer's not taunting us anymore.

He's in the building.

And he's not here for a message.

He's here to finish something.

Chapter 34

My gun is steady, but my heart isn't. I edge toward the hallway that leads to the back of the apartment, the hardwood creaking under my boots like a traitor.

Behind me, Robert breathes shallow, rattled. I signal with a hand—stay low, stay quiet.

That *click* I heard? It wasn't imagination. The back window's got a cheap latch. Easy to pop open with a knife. I've seen it done a dozen times.

And someone's using that entrance now.

I reach the corner and flatten against the wall, weapon up, flashlight in my off-hand. The light from the living room barely reaches this far—shadows stack in the corners like waiting ghosts.

Another sound—closer now.

A shoe against tile.

Bathroom? Kitchen?

I twist the knob on the flashlight, cutting the darkness with a narrow beam. The back window is wide open. Curtains flap like they're trying to escape.

No one in sight.

But the breeze is wrong.

Too cold.

Too sharp.

It carried something with it.

I step in, light sweeping the walls.

There's a long scratch across the counter. Fresh. Metal on stone.

And something else.

A smear. Rust-red. Not blood—grease maybe, or ink. But it streaks toward the hallway leading to the bedrooms.

I exhale through my nose. My voice is low and flat.

"Come out now. Hands where I can see them. You move, I shoot."

Silence.

Then—*a voice.*

Low. Whispered from behind the pantry door.

"You're late... detective."

My spine stiffens.

I pivot instantly, flashlight and weapon raised. "Step out. Now."

Nothing.

But then—

Something *flies* at my face.

I duck. It's a small object—a photo. It flutters to the floor like a leaf.

I step on it to pin it.

It's Sabrina.

Bound. Blindfolded. Kneeling in front of a digital clock.

Countdown flashing:

00:12:34

A handwritten message scrawled on the bottom in red ink:

"This is how long you have left."

My blood turns to ice.

I raise the flashlight again, and the pantry door slams shut from the inside.

I lunge, shoulder first.

Crash!

The door bursts open.

Empty.

Just canned food and darkness.

But there's a hole in the wall.

A crawl space—small, tight, carved out behind the cabinets.

He's using the structure itself to move.

I shout at Robert. "Call this in—NOW! He was *in* your walls!"

Robert stammers something, fumbling with the phone. I tear back through the living room, toward the fire escape window.

The metal stairs are swaying.

He's gone.

But he left something behind.

I spot it lying on the windowsill.

A watch.

Not just any watch.

Sabrina's.

I grab it and press the button on the side.

It beeps once.

And flashes:

00:12:17

Still counting down.

Whatever this is, it's more than a message.

It's a game.

And I just got dealt the next hand.

Chapter 35

The door creaks open just enough for a pair of tired blue eyes to peek through.

"Wyatt Haller?" I flash my badge. "Detective Stanley. Got a few questions. You got a minute?"

He blinks like he's buffering, then glances down the hallway. Not toward danger—toward escape. He's thinking about it.

"I'm not here to cuff you," I add. "Just need to talk."

His shoulders drop, and after a second's hesitation, he pulls the door open. "Yeah, sure. Come in, I guess."

His apartment smells like cheap detergent, microwaved food, and desperation. There's a plate of half-eaten spaghetti on the coffee table next to a muted rerun of *Montel*. And there, hanging on a chair like some trophy, is a black suit—pressed, prepped, and perfect.

"You dressing for a funeral or a future?" I ask.

He chuckles awkwardly. "Nah, dude—it's for an interview. Tomorrow. Accounting firm, accounts payable, or whatever. Finally got a callback. Took me like—what— thirty resumes and a nervous breakdown?"

I nod, stepping further inside. "Good for you. You look ready."

He crosses his arms, trying to play it cool but failing. "So, uh... why are you here?"

I gesture toward the blinking light on his answering machine. "You got a card earlier. Caught Security Services. Ring a bell?"

His brow furrows. "Wait... yeah. It just fell out of my shirt pocket. Kinda weird, 'cause I don't even remember putting it there."

I reach into my coat and pull out an evidence bag. Inside is another copy of the same card. Same font. Same number.

"This one came from the closet of a murder victim," I tell him. "Sabrina Blake. You know her?"

Wyatt's face drains white like someone just pulled the plug. He shakes his head fast. "No. No, dude—I've never heard that name before."

"The killer took Sabrina last night and left a message taped to the wall. Bloody. Taunting."

He shifts on his heels. "Okay, yeah, but... what does that have to do with me?"

"You worked at a burger place on Plymouth Road. Managed by Ricky Sanders. Ring a bell?"

He nods slowly. "Yeah, that guy was a—uh—kind of a tool. Always on my case, cutting hours, acting like he was running a five-star steakhouse."

"You were fired after a fight. Witnesses said you snapped."

"Yeah, I mean... okay, yeah, I lost it a little. But I didn't like to hurt him or anything. I—look, man, he shoved me. I shoved back. End of story."

I step toward the suit hanging up. "Mind if I check this?"

He raises his hands like, "Sure, go ahead."

I reach into the inside pocket and feel paper. Thin. Smooth.

I pull it out slowly.

A photograph.

Sabrina. Tied. Blindfolded. Kneeling beside a digital clock flashing red:

00:07:03

Below it, one sentence in dripping red ink:

"He's next. You know who."

I turn the photo so Wyatt can see it. He stares. Stares like the air's been sucked out of his lungs.

"Dude... I—what the hell is that? That was *in* the suit?"

I nod.

"I swear, man, I didn't put that there. I didn't even check the pockets."

I believe him. His reaction isn't rehearsed—he's genuinely shaking. I slip the photo into an evidence bag.

My radio crackles to life.

"Detective Stanley, this is Officer Andre. We just got an anonymous call. Said to check the abandoned convent near Livernois in Detroit. Said—'he won't live to see the sun.'"

I freeze.

Wyatt whispers, "Ricky... that's gotta be about Ricky, right?"

I nod once, slow and grim.

Wyatt backs toward the couch again, whispering, "Man, this is like... this is like something out of a horror movie."

I'm already halfway to the door. "Hope your suit fits."

"Why?"

I pause with my hand on the knob.

"Because if we don't find Ricky in time... you're wearing it to his funeral."

Wendell Peeples

I yank the door open, storm into the hallway, and vanish into the dark—

—with *six minutes left on the clock.*

Chapter 36

The afternoon air is thick with tension as I lean against the precinct's third-floor window, watching traffic crawl below. Andre steps into the room, coffee in one hand, folder in the other.

"So," he says, placing the folder on the table between us. "Where do we start?"

I exhale slowly, my thoughts running like wildfire. "We've got six persons of interest. Six names circling this case like vultures. And every one of them has something to hide."

Andre raises a brow. "Go on."

I start with Robert. "Quiet. Calculated. Always around, always listening. He plays the peacemaker, but there's something about him. When Ian almost offed himself,

Robert was the first on the scene. Right place, right time or too right?"

"You think he's manipulating the group?"

"I think he knows more than he says. Maybe pulling strings. Maybe cleaning up."

Andre nods slowly. "Next?"

"Shawn," I say. "Always in the middle of everything, but never takes the heat. The guy runs interference. Makes calls. Sends people places. He's like a walking alibi factory. He's either the glue keeping things together or the shadow behind it all."

"Ian?"

I rub the bridge of my nose. "That kid's a mess. Tried to kill himself. Got dumped. No job. But, Andre, what if it wasn't just the girl or the pills? What if it was guilt? He saw something. Maybe did something. He mentioned someone in a winter coat that night. Eighty degrees. Something is not right."

Andre scribbles that down. "Winter coat. Got it."

"Then there's Wyatt. Clean cut. Degree-holder. But something's off. We found a photo of Sabrina in his suit pocket—blindfolded, tied up, next to a countdown clock. He swears he didn't put it there."

"Do you believe him?"

"I believe he's scared. Someone's setting him up—or using him as a delivery boy. Either way, the photo didn't end up in his pocket by magic."

Andre leans in. "Lexi?"

I hesitate. "She's the wild card. Sabrina's old roommate. Always around drama. Used to be close with Dominic, until she wasn't. And she hated Gina's jealousy, maybe. She hasn't returned a single one of our calls."

"And Dominic?"

"Dominic's dangerous. Charming when he wants to be. Controlling when he doesn't get his way. Sabrina's brother. The last one to have the keys to her apartment. But here's the kicker—his name's on a security company we found tied to that photo: Caught Security Services."

Andre freezes. "He owns it?"

"Or someone's using his name. I checked the state filings—Dominic's name is on the LLC registration. We traced the briefcase Ian left at Olsen's office. Guess what was stenciled on the front?"

Andre breathes, "Caught Security."

I nod. "And now Ian's freaking out, realizing it wasn't his to begin with."

Andre stands, pacing. "So what are we saying? Did Dominic plant the briefcase? That he's orchestrating something?"

"Or he's cleaning something up. Either way, this all ties back to him—and if we don't move fast, we're going to lose our window."

My phone vibrates.

One new message.

I open it.

A photo.

Of Robert.

Bound.

Blindfolded.

Clock reads: 00:59:04

Beneath it, a new message:

"Round two. Tick tock, Detective."

I look at Andre, my stomach turning to ice.

"They've taken Robert."

Andre goes still. "This killer's not just playing games anymore."

"No," I say, grabbing my coat. "He's already made his next move."

And we're an hour behind.

Chapter 37

Andre stands by the window, arms crossed, watching the storm roll in. Thunder grumbles low across the city like a warning we're too slow to understand.

I pace the floor, shoes scuffing the worn tile, files spread across the table like the pieces of a puzzle we keep forcing into the wrong damn places.

"Let's go over it again," I say. My voice sounds like gravel, raw from sleepless nights and burned-out cigarettes. Six persons of interest. Six stories that almost make sense."

Andre turns, eyes tired but sharp. "Robert. The loyal one. But maybe too loyal."

I nod. "He's got access, a clean record, and a calm surface. But something about him doesn't sit right. The way he showed up at Ian's apartment before the paramedics? Almost too fast."

Andre shrugs. "He said Shawn called him."

I pick up a file and toss it on the table. "Which brings us to Shawn. The connector. Always knows where the fire is—but never gets burned."

"He's charming," Andre says. "Too charming. And he was the first one Ian called when he took the pills. That's a deep level of trust—or manipulation."

I point to the following file. "Ian. Self-destructive, depressed, chaotic. He's the perfect fall guy. But maybe that's the point. Maybe someone made him the perfect fall guy."

"He did mention seeing someone in a winter coat the night of the party," Andre adds. "Eighty degrees out. That ain't nothing."

I glance at the board. "Wyatt. Quiet. Smart. Too smart. And that photo of Sabrina stuffed in his suit jacket? That wasn't just a message. That was a signature. It wasn't left for him—it was left for us."

Andre grimaces. "Then there's Lexi."

"Yeah," I mutter. "The wild card. We don't know what she knows—or what she's capable of. She hasn't come forward once. That makes me nervous."

Andre clears his throat, voice low. "That leaves Dominic. Sabrina's brother. Ex-military. Discharged under 'questionable circumstances.' That apartment key—he never reported it missing."

I tap my fingers against the table. Something's off. The same itch I get before a case takes a turn. I scan the photos. Each face stares back at me like it knows a secret.

"John," Andre says cautiously, "you okay?"

"No," I reply, staring at the board. "Because something's missing."

"What do you mean?"

I step closer to the wall, eyes narrowing. "We keep circling these six. Over and over. But it doesn't fit. It's not six. It's seven."

Andre looks up sharply. "Seven? Who's the seventh?"

I slowly pull a folder from under the stack. A name I didn't want to see again. A name I buried because it didn't belong. But now.

I dropped it on the table.

SAM.

Andres stares at it. "You're kidding. He was cleared."

"Was he?" I whisper. "Or were we just too distracted?"

Andre flips the folder open. "He was at the Ring Zone that night. He left early."

"No," I say, heart thudding. "He didn't leave. He watched. And we missed him."

Outside, lightning flashes, briefly illuminating the board. Sam's face—smiling, forgettable—now feels like the devil in disguise.

I step back, pulse rising. "He's been one step ahead this entire time."

Andre looks at me, eyes wide. "Then what the hell is he planning now?"

The radio crackles behind us. A voice cuts through the static.

"Detective Stanley. We just got a call. Anonymous. The caller said, 'Check the old school on Burlingame. Clock's almost up."

Andre and I lock eyes.

"Clock's almost up," he echoes.

I grab my coat.

"We're out of time," I say, bolting for the door.

The wind howls as we step into the night—and I swear, somewhere in the dark, Sam is watching.

And smiling.

.

Chapter 38

I grip the wheel tighter than I should. My knuckles ache, but I don't loosen up. Andre sits beside me, silent, loading his weapon with clean, deliberate clicks. The city passes by in streaks of light and fog, but my mind is already inside that building.

The old school on Burlingame.

Three stories of forgotten halls and broken windows. Condemned. Boarded up for years. The kind of place you only hear about in ghost stories—or murder cases.

"Clock's almost up," Andre mutters again. "Bastard's playing games."

"No," I say. "He's setting the board. And we're walking straight into it."

We pull up to the curb. I kill the headlights. The school rises in the dark like a monument to failure. The chain-link fence rusted open—a single floodlight flickers above the side entrance.

I step out, my boots crunching on the glass.

The night is dead silent.

No wind. No cars.

Even the city's holding its breath.

Andre and I slip through the fence and approach the door, guns drawn. I nod to him. He yanks the handle—unlocked.

Figures.

The door creaks open into a black corridor that smells like mold and burnt paper. I flick on my flashlight and sweep it across the walls. Torn posters. Lockers hanging open like mouths. A child's drawing was still taped to one of the doors—faded stick figures under a sun that never rose.

"I'll cover left," Andre whispers.

I nod. We split.

Each step echoes. My light catches empty desks stacked against the wall, a toppled chalkboard, a ragged shoe with no foot in sight.

Then I see it.

On the linoleum floor, smeared in something dark—

"WELCOME BACK."

Paint? Blood?

I don't check. I already know.

I press my radio. "Andre. First floor, east wing. He's here."

His voice crackles back. "Copy. I think I found something, too. Second floor. Room 212. There's a trail."

I hesitate. "Blood?"

A pause.

"Clocks."

I freeze.

"What kind of clocks?"

"Dozens of 'em. Broken, ticking, some with wires. But they're all stopped at one time."

My breath hitches.

"7:03."

That was the time in the photo. Sabrina. Bound. Kneeling. Countdown running.

I start toward the staircase. "Stay where you are. I'm coming up."

I make it to the second floor. Wood splinters under my boots. Every step sounds like it's waking the dead.

Andre stands outside Room 212, his flashlight aimed at the door.

I reach him.

"What's inside?" I whisper.

"See for yourself."

I push the door open.

And I stop cold.

The walls are covered in clocks.

Dozens of them. Hanging from nails, resting on chairs, some shattered, some pristine.

All stuck at 7:03.

One of them suddenly ticks.

Just once.

Then silence.

In the center of the room sits an old school desk. On it, a Polaroid photo.

I step forward and pick it up.

It's me.

Taken from behind. Standing in front of the crime scene at Sabrina's apartment.

My blood runs cold.

There's something scrawled on the back in red marker:

"HE'S BEEN IN YOUR SHADOW SINCE DAY ONE."

Andre looks at me, his face pale. "John... what does that mean?"

But I can't answer.

Because I feel it—cold air curling through the room, and a low beep echoing through the vents above us.

Tick.

Then another.

Tick.

Then a whisper.

"Detective..."

We spin, weapons drawn—

And the lights go out.

Darkness swallows us whole.

And somewhere in the black

A door creaks open.

Chapter 39

The lights are gone. Pitch black. Only the dying wheeze of a power relay humming somewhere behind the walls.

"Andre?" I hiss.

"I'm here," he says—closer than I expected. I hear the metal click of his safety being thumbed off. "Don't move. We're not alone anymore."

No kidding.

Something shifts in the hall just outside the classroom. A shuffle. A creak. Maybe footsteps. Maybe something worse.

I sweep the flashlight—dead.

My thumb taps it. Nothing. Battery's gone.

"Cover me," I whisper, sliding toward the doorway—
my heart pounds in my chest.

We step into the hallway.

The clocks have followed us.

Not literally, but the sound.

Tick, tick, tick.

It's faint, but I can hear it—inside the walls, maybe the
vents. Like something alive is crawling between the bricks,
carrying time like a virus.

We move slow. I take the front. Andre covers the rear.

The corridor splits ahead. Left leads to the gym.
Right—an old faculty lounge. Both doors hang open.

"Split?" Andre whispers.

I nod. "Two minutes. If you don't hear my voice, call
it in."

He taps his shoulder radio and disappears into the gym.

I move right.

The lounge smells like mildew and dust. I step inside,
weapon raised. My eyes adjust—shapes emerge. A coffee
machine half-eaten by rust. A sofa draped in a moldy
blanket. And pinned to the wall beside the vending
machine—

A map.

I step closer.

It's a floor plan of the school. Every room is marked in
red, except for one.

Basement boiler room.

That one's circled in black.

Taped over the map is another photo.

A classroom—Room 109.

Kids' desks. A chalkboard. Scribbled across the blackboard in chalk:

"HE'S WAITING."

I yank the photo down just as Andre bursts in behind me.

"John—we've got a problem."

"What now?"

He's breathing hard. "There's a body in the gym. Hung up like a puppet. Old, decomposed—but dressed like a janitor. Keys still on his belt. Name tag says. Sam Baxter."

My blood turns to ash.

Baxter was the original custodian here. Vanished seven years ago. The building shut down after a gas leak. Everyone said he just walked out one day and never came back.

But he never left.

Not really.

I hold up the floor plan. "He's got a base in the boiler room."

Andre nods, eyes wide. "Then that's where we go."

We head down.

The stairs creak with every step. The air thickens with the scent of rot and mold. Halfway down, we hear it again—

Tick. Tick. Tick.

Faster now. Louder.

It's coming from the pipes.

We reach the basement landing. The boiler room door is shut. A single chain wraps around the handle, locked securely in place.

Andre draws the bolt cutters from his pack and snaps them in two.

The door creaks open.

The smell is overwhelming.

Darkness. Wetness. Rusted tools were scattered across the benches. A flickering bulb dangles from the ceiling like a noose.

And in the center of the room—

A mannequin.

Dressed in a black security uniform.

Taped to its chest: a name tag that reads "Caught Security."

And around its neck

A digital timer.

It flashes.

00:02:17

I freeze.

Then I hear it.

From the shadows behind the furnace—

A whisper.

"Detective... you're late."

I swing the light and weapon—

But there's no one there.

The timer ticks down.

Andre is already moving. "John—we've got to go. Now."

I take one last look at the mannequin.

Its mouth opens.

Something inside it blinks red.

00:01:44

We bolt.

Up the stairs, through the halls, out into the night—

And behind us, the school breathes.

Like it's alive.

Like Sam is in its walls.

Watching.

Waiting.

Planning his next move.

Chapter 40

We hit the stairwell like ghosts with guns drawn. Every creak of these warped steps feels like a threat. The darkness down here isn't just the absence of light—it's presence. Heavy. Watching.

Andre moves ahead, sweeping corners with his flashlight. Mine's back on, flickering at the edges, barely holding charge. I can feel it—the charge in the air, like something's waiting for us.

We reach the boiler room again. The ticking's gone now.

Replaced by a sound I never expected—

A cough.

Ragged. Wet. Human.

I hold up a fist. Andre freezes behind me.

Then we hear it—muffled crying.

We broke down the door.

My light catches something in the far corner.

Two figures.

Bound. Bloodied. Eyes wide.

Robert. And Sabrina.

"Jesus..." Andre whispers behind me.

I move fast. "Robert. It's me. John. You're safe now."

He flinches, squinting against the light. His lips are cracked, dried blood at his temple. Sabrina's head rolls toward me, barely conscious. Duct tape across her mouth. Rope around her wrists.

I slice through the restraints.

She collapses into me.

"Get EMTs. Now," I bark to Andre.

He's already on his radio, stepping back toward the stairwell.

Robert grips my wrist, trembling. "He... he was here. He never left. He was wearing a mask."

I lean closer. "What kind of mask?"

"Plain. White. Like, like a mannequin. No eyes. Just holes."

I feel my stomach drop.

"The mask was wrong," Sabrina rasps, her voice cracked. "It didn't move, but it felt like he was... smiling."

A door creaks behind us.

Andre spins, gun raised. "Who's there?!"

No answer.

Only silence.

Then—

Clink. Clink. Clink.

Something metal hits the floor just outside the room. Like a coin. Or a spent shell casing.

I rise, gun ready.

Sabrina clutches my arm. "He said... he's still here. Watching."

Andre meets my eyes.

And then we hear it—

The locker doors in the hallway all slam shut at once.

BOOM-BOOM-BOOM—like a wave of metal thunder.

Andre grabs my shoulder. "We've got to move them now."

"No." I scan the room, my pulse pounding. "This was planned. He wanted us here. He wanted us to find them."

I reach down. Robert's hand is clenched into a fist.

"Open it," I whisper.

He's shaking. Slowly unfolds his fingers.

In his palm, a piece of torn paper.

I take it and read:

"You're still chasing shadows. The real face hasn't even turned around yet."

And then—

A whisper from the ceiling vent above us.

Not a voice.

A laugh.

Cold. Mechanical.

He's in the building.

Chapter 41

The vents above us groan again. That laugh still echoes in my bones. Not loud. Not human. Just enough to make the hairs on the back of my neck stand up like soldiers who know they're surrounded.

Andre covers Robert and Sabrina, still shaking, still bleeding. I step out into the corridor.

Every locker door is wide open now. Like mouths.

I sweep my light across the hallway. Nothing. No footprints. No shadow. Just the sound of my own breath tight in my chest.

And then I see it.

The fire alarm switch.

It's missing its cover—yanked. But the alarm never rang.

That's not possible.

Unless someone rewired it.

I feel it now—not fear. Not even rage.

Control.

He's controlling the room, the temperature, and the lights.

He's watching. He's been watching.

From the boiler room to this hallway—this isn't just a school. It's his stage.

And we're performing exactly the way he wants us to.

"John," Andre calls from behind me, urgency in his voice. "You need to see this."

I rush back in.

He's holding Sabrina's torn sleeve. Embedded in the fabric, so small you'd miss it, is a metal sliver—flat and etched with something faint.

I squint.

A GPS chip.

My blood turns cold. I've seen this tech before—military-level tracking.

He tagged her.

Andre turns it over. There's a brand name.

"Catchlight Industries."

Never heard of it.

I pull out my phone and punch in a request to forensics. "Run this company. See what comes back. Fast."

Sabrina murmurs something.

I kneel beside her. "What is it?"

Her lips tremble. "He said that we'd never see his real face... only the items he leaves behind."

A reflection.

I turn the chip over again.

It's not just a tracker.

There's a number on it.

003.

"Robert," I say, grabbing his shoulder. "Did he say anything to you?"

He nods slowly. "Only... 'You're number four.'"

I stand. "He's counting. He's got a list."

Andre looks at me. "And if they're three and four..."

"Then two's already gone," I whisper.

And one?

The worst thought hits me like a punch to the throat.

What if I'm number one?

The radio crackles in my ear.

"Detective Stanley, you're not gonna believe this. A package just arrived at your desk. No return address. Just a black envelope inside. And it's ticking."

I freeze.

Andre looks at me, wide-eyed. "You think it's a bomb?"

"No," I mutter, heart hammering now. "It's a message."

The kind you only send when you know exactly where your enemy is.

And exactly what time he'll get back.

Andre says what I'm thinking.

"He's not running from us."

"No," I say grimly, turning toward the exit.

"He's leading us."

And every step we take is part of his blueprint.

Chapter 42

t's hot enough to make asphalt sweat. June in Chicago is a punch to the lungs—sun glaring, humidity clinging like guilt. People are everywhere, pouring into Lake Shore like ants around a melting popsicle. Radios clash—rap on one side, house on the other—bodies grinding, drinking, flexing.

But I'm not here to party.

I kill the engine and sit low in the unmarked Crown Vic. From this spot, I've got eyes on Trina's townhouse. She just pulled in with her friend Katie. Country twang and corporate gloss, an odd pairing, but this case has taught me that opposites don't just attract—they conspire.

They're laughing now, climbing the steps. I click my recorder on. It's not officially legal surveillance. But I've got a gut feeling, and my gut hasn't failed me yet.

They disappear inside.

Minutes pass. I cracked the window. Faint voices bleed through.

"You got vodka, beer, anything?" Katie's voice twangs out.

Trina replies, "It's a bar in my house, honey. Help yourself."

More laughter. Then silence. I lean closer.

"There's something about this place," Katie says, her voice dropping. "Like I've been here before."

"What do you mean?" Trina sounds unsettled now.

Katie hesitates. "Angela... remember her? She lived in a house like this. Same setup. Except we came in through the front."

Angela. Another name from my list. One of the early victims.

"This isn't the same house," Trina replies quickly, too quickly.

Katie's not buying it. "But the address..."

A pause.

"I said drop it!" Trina snaps.

Then the lights inside go out.

My stomach drops.

I throw the door open, already moving. The sun's dipping behind the skyline, casting the neighborhood in rust and shadow. I'm halfway to the porch when I hear the first scream.

High. Piercing.

Female.

I bolt up the stairs, gun drawn. The front door's locked. I circle left, catch a flash in the side window. Movement. Struggle.

I slam my shoulder into the door once. Twice. It cracks open just as another scream shatters the air.

I step inside and stop cold.

Blood. Everywhere. On the walls. The floor. On the ceiling fan, spinning lazily like a forgotten carousel of death.

A body lies twisted near the entryway. Blonde hair. Katie.

Her eyes are wide, mouth open in a silent scream.

I move forward slowly, my gun raised.

The hallway stretches long and quiet. I glance left. A red trail smears across the tile—drag marks.

Then I hear it.

Breathing.

Not panicked. Controlled. Close.

I press my back against the wall and inch forward.

The closet door creaks.

I aim.

Nothing.

Then—

Footsteps behind me.

I spin—

Too late.

A shadow crashes into me—heavy, fast, deliberate. I hit the wall hard; my vision was swimming—my gun slid across the floor.

By the time I recover, he's gone.

Whoever he is, he's playing games.

I rush back outside. The alley's empty. The street was silent.

Except

There, scratched into the side of my car window.

"YOU'RE NEXT."

The letters are smeared in blood.

And underneath them, taped to the glass, is a photo.

It's me.

Standing at my nephew Raymond's gravesite.

And in the corner of the frame

A reflection.

Someone wearing a ski mask.

Watching.

Chapter 43

It's been three months since the third body was found, and still, the air inside Becky's office smells like fear masked by lavender plug-ins. I lean against the stairwell rail across from HR, a Styrofoam cup of bitter station coffee in hand. Lance felt better because I was there—I'm not on official duty. But something's off, and I feel it deep in my bones.

Becky's back on the job. She walks the hall with a new title—HR Generalist now, fifteen thousand richer, though no one's celebrating. Not after three of her co-workers ended up zipped up in coroner bags.

Women no longer walk alone. They move in pairs like schoolgirls afraid of the dark. Security guards tail them to their cars like silent bodyguards with sidearms. But I know how killers think—and this one's watching. Waiting.

Becky slips into her office, humming along to some soft pop song playing from her phone. I catch a glimpse of her in the reflection of a wall-mounted poster—reapplying red lipstick, fluffing her hair. She's trying to hold it together.

Then her phone rings.

"Becky, we have a nine-thirty meeting today in the conference room. Bring your laptop with you, and we'll see you there," Lance's voice echoes out from her desk.

"All right!" she chirps back, snapping out of the mirror daze.

I trail behind her as she walks down the hallway toward the conference room, staying back enough to go unnoticed. She's trying to put on a brave face, but her shoulders are tight. Eyes darting.

She walks into the room and sits at the far end of the long table beneath the projector screen. More department heads start to file in. The room hums with low conversation, nervous chuckles. Everyone's pretending to be okay, but I can see the cracks.

Lance and the HR Director come in next. His assistant fumbles with the projector, as if his hands are too sweaty to function.

"Good morning, everyone," Lance begins, projecting authority he doesn't feel. The screen flickers to life behind him, showing a bar chart of department staffing levels. "We know everyone's still dealing with... well, everything. Counseling is still available if you need it."

Translation: Don't fall apart on company time.

I duck into the maintenance hall beside the conference room—thin walls. Good acoustics.

"We need to fill positions in each area..." he drones on.

But I'm not listening to him anymore. I hear something else.

Two women are whispering. Close. In the hallway just behind the glass.

I inch toward the sound.

It's Becky and another woman—I think her name's Carla. Becky's voice is barely a murmur.

"I swear to you, Carla... I saw someone. Outside my building. Two nights ago."

"You sure it wasn't security?" Carla whispers, her voice brittle.

"No. He was standing still, just standing there. Across the street. Watching."

A long silence.

"He was wearing a mask," Becky says finally. "Not a COVID one. Like a ski mask."

My heart skips.

"I thought it was my imagination," she continues. "But last night, there was a note under my windshield."

Carla gasps. "What did it say?"

Becky's voice is paper-thin. "It just said: 'You're still on the list.'"

I press my hand against the wall to steady myself. My fingers twitch toward my phone, recording on instinct.

Carla says something about going to the police. Becky cuts her off.

"No. I don't want to die like the others."

That's when I realize—I'm not here by accident.

I'm here because he wanted me here.

And then I hear it. A phone buzzes.

A third voice, low and guttural, not belonging to either of the women. From behind them.

"You shouldn't be talking about the list."

Then a scream.

I burst out of the hallway—gun drawn, badge flashing. But the corridor's empty. The conference room door bangs open—Lance yelling something.

No sign of Becky. Or Carla.

Just a trail of lipstick smeared on the wall, and a note taped beside it.

All it says is:

"I warned her."

Chapter 44

I stood in the empty hallway, my eyes fixed on the note taped just beneath the red smear.
"I warned her."
No signature. No initials. Just bold, slanted handwriting, pressed deep into the page. The scent of Becky's perfume still lingers in the air—sweet, powdery. But she's gone. Both she and Carla have vanished like ghosts slipping through a crack in the floor.

I radio, Andre. "I need eyes on all exits. Lock the stairwells. Sweep every floor—now."
I don't wait for a response. I tear the note from the wall and slip it into an evidence bag. Then I head straight to HR—Becky's office. Something in my gut tells me we're missing something. Something obvious.

Inside her office, it's neat—too neat. The blinds are half open, sunlight stretching across her desk like a silent alarm. I sit down in her chair and open her top drawer. Pens. Makeup. Sticky notes. A folded letter addressed to "Angela M."

I freeze.

Angela. As in Angela Dorsey, the second woman murdered in this case. The one found in the apartment with the blood trail leading to the closet. The same Angela Becky claimed she barely knew.

I unfold the letter slowly. It's dated March 17th, two weeks before Angela's death.

Becky, thank you for the wine and for always being there to listen. I know I've made mistakes, but someone's watching me. I don't know how much longer I can pretend I don't see him. Please keep what I told you between us. Promise me you won't tell anyone—not even Lance.

A chill creeps down my spine. Becky lied to us. She knew Angela. Not only knew her—they were close. Close enough for wine and secrets.

I keep digging.

I log into her desktop. Her calendar is synced. There was a dinner meeting with Angela, just five days before Angela was killed. And another with someone named "R.S." That's either a person... or initials.

Then I find a message flagged in her inbox from a private email:

Subject line: "Still think you're safe?"

No body text. Just a video attachment.

I hesitate. Then click.

The screen fills with grainy footage from a security cam, shot at night. A woman, head down, walking toward her car. She's wearing the same outfit Becky wore this morning.

But it's not today. The timestamp is from three days ago, at 9:12 PM.

In the corner of the screen, a figure steps out from the shadows. A tall man. Masked. He walks behind her and watches.

The video cuts out.

I shut the laptop and immediately had to call Andre. "Becky knew Angela. She's been lying to us."

"You sure?"

"I've got a letter, calendar entries, and a surveillance video sent to her three days ago. The killer's been taunting her. Watching her."

"What about that name—R.S.?"

"I'm working on it."

I hang up and flip the letter over. There's a faint imprint on the back. Someone wrote something beneath it on the pad.

I grab a pencil and start shading the indentation.

Words slowly appear:

"Ask her what happened in Michigan."

My pulse spikes.

Michigan.

That's where my nephew, Raymond, was murdered. The first body. The one that started this.

Deadly Oath

All this time, I thought Raymond was just in the wrong place at the wrong time. But now
Now I'm not so sure.

And if Becky knew Angela, and both women feared the same man. Then the killer's been playing a longer game than I ever imagined.

I step out of Becky's office. The hallway is too quiet. The building hums with fake calm.

Then a single text pings my phone.
Blocked number.
"Becky's story ends tonight. Stop chasing ghosts, Stanley."

I take off running.

Chapter 45

'm parked two blocks down, the engine idling, the windows cracked just enough to hear the soft hiss of static through my earpiece. Andre's house looms in the distance, half-swallowed by shadows and porch light. I tap the side of my phone, double-checking the signal.

The line clicks. Voices come through—clear.

Andre shuts the door behind him. I hear the soft thud of it closing, the jingle of keys, the faint scrape of a badge tossed onto the counter. He sighs, deep and tired. The kind of breath a man exhales when the world's been riding his shoulders for too long.

Then her voice slips through the wire like honey.

"I haven't seen you in a week since I went on vacation," Mia says, playfully. Smooth like molasses. "So I'd better take advantage of this situation."

Andre laughs, low and unguarded. "Aww, somebody missed me."

He sounds lighter already. But that's not why I'm listening.

"They got you workin' like a runaway mule," Mia murmurs, wrapping herself around him in my mind. "We don't even see each other like we should. It ain't right."

"I know," Andre says. There's weight in his voice again. "Feels like I ain't been home in months."

He's not wrong. This case has turned all our lives inside out.

I hear her robe swish as she walks toward the bathroom.

"Let me go change into something a little more... persuasive."

He chuckles, loosens his tie. I hear the bed creak under his weight.

"You done filled out," Mia says, eyes probably roaming over him. "Them arms lookin' dangerous."

She's trying to tease the stress out of him. I get it. I also know he wanted me to hear this. That's why he let the phone stay on.

They settle into something softer. Their voices drop. The conversation shifts.

"Have you talked to our son lately?" Andre asks.

Mia exhales. "That boy acts like his phone doesn't dial home. We used to be close, you know?"

Andre nods in response—I can hear it in the silence. "He doesn't call me either. Might be life just hittin' him fast."

Then comes the question I've been waiting for.

"You still working that case? The one that's got the city shook?"

"Yeah," Andre says, rubbing something—his temples, probably. "John's been gettin' a lot of tips. He's sharp— real sharp. Ain't afraid to dig into things."

He says it loud enough for me to hear. Maybe to remind me I'm not in this alone.

Then her voice lowers. "I'm not gon lie to you. This whole thing got me watchin' my back. They had security walking us to our cars. I don't like living like this, Dre. You gotta catch this monster."

"You got me," he tells her. "Ain't nothin' gon' happen to you."

Another pause. A drawer opens. I hear the click of metal.

"And if it does, this lil friend right here gon' make sure I walk out standin'," she says, half-joking. The grin in her voice doesn't hide the fear beneath it.

They laugh. But there's something hollow behind the sound. Then she adds, "Our daughter's scared too."

He sighs again. "We're close. Closer than we've ever been. I can feel it."

"You promise?" she asks.

"I promise the case gon' end. I might not be the one to catch him, but someone will."

She exhales slowly. Let's herself believe it. "Then come on. Let's get some sleep."

"Good night, baby."

"Good night."

The lamp clicks off.

Silence.

Then—

Buzz.

I sit up straighter in the car. Another buzz.

Andre steps into the hallway—I can hear his footsteps, slow and heavy.

He mutters under his breath. "Blocked number."

Then the line goes dead.

Seconds pass. I stare through the windshield, heart ticking like a metronome. Then my phone lights up.

Incoming message from Andre.

"She's not who she says she is. Go back to the first body. You missed something."

Attached: a photo. Crime scene. Angela Dorsey.

But there's something different in this version. A figure. Someone in the background.

Not the killer. Not the witness. Someone else. Someone we have already interviewed.

I lean back in the seat, cold creeping over my spine. I stare at the image, zooming in on that shadowed face.

Andre's voice comes through again, low, shaken.

"Someone on our team's hiding something, John."

I already know.

Because I can feel it, too.

And I'm not going to sleep until I find out who it is.

Chapter 46

I can't sleep. Not after that photo Andre sent. Angela Dorsey's body sprawled across that hallway—twisted, lifeless. But that's not what's keeping me up. It's what's behind her. A blurred silhouette, tucked into the shadows just beyond the crime scene tape. Watching.

Not the killer. Not any uniform I recognize. But I *know* that shape. I *know* that posture.

I grab my badge, throw on my jacket, and head out the door.

When I pull into the precinct lot, Andre's car is already there, engine still warm. He's been here a while. My phone buzzes—his message again, still sitting there: "We've been looking in the wrong direction."

Inside, the place is dead quiet. Just the night shift manning the front desk, half-asleep behind a cold cup of coffee. I nod, flash my ID, and make my way toward the records room.

The second I open the door, I hear it—papers shifting, drawers sliding, someone rifling through files with urgency. Andre's in there, hunched over a table, buried in folders and evidence bags. His face is pale. Focused.

"John," he says without looking up, "you need to see this."

He pulls out a printed photo and slaps it onto the table next to Angela's case file. I lean in.

There she is—Angela—frozen in death. But there, in the background, just beyond the crime scene tape... a shadow. Blurry. Almost lost in the grain. But the angle's wrong. That photo wasn't taken by any of our guys.

Andre adjusts the contrast on his laptop. The pixels stutter, but something catches—an employee badge. The letter *L*—just barely visible.

"Matches the company ID format," he says. "L for Lance. Her boss."

I blink. "Lance was in that morning meeting three days after her murder."

He nods. "Gave a speech about 'protecting the company culture.' Told staff to stick together. Swore he barely knew her."

"And yet she called someone at 10:16 p.m. the night she died," I say, piecing it together. "That call went to

Rebecca. The same Rebecca who swore they only spoke in the breakroom."

"Emergency contact," Andre mutters. "Nobody puts a casual coworker down as that."

He steps back from the table, breath tight. "Someone's lying, John. And that picture? That wasn't in any of the files Jenkins gave us. Wasn't leaked to the press either."

"So whoever took it..." I start.

"...was there before the cops showed," he finishes.

I nod, jaw clenched. "Which means they were watching the whole damn thing."

Andre closes the laptop slowly, like something inside it might explode. Then, just as he turns to grab the rest of the file—

The lights flicker.

Then go out.

Total black.

We both freeze.

A low hum from the emergency light above the door, but it doesn't kick on. Backup power's not working. That doesn't happen.

I reach for my holster.

Andre whispers, "You hear that?"

Footsteps.

Not ours.

And they're getting closer.

From the far end of the hallway. Someone slow. Intentional. The sound of boots against tile. Too calm for a janitor. Too quiet for patrol.

Then a voice—behind us, near the ceiling vents, like it's riding the shadows.

"Detective Andre..."

Andre spins around.

I drop into a crouch, gun drawn. My back hits the file cabinet.

Silence.

Then—I feel it.

A hand.

Cold and steady.

Gripping my shoulder from behind.

Chapter 47

freeze. That creak isn't just a sound—it's a threat dragging its nails down my spine.

Gun raised, I pivot toward the stairwell, breath low and steady. The hallway behind me hums with the faint electric buzz of the monitor still playing that damn clip—Angela's body, the badge, the timestamp from *yesterday*.

This precinct has a basement.

Of course it does.

But no one uses it. Or at least... no one is *supposed* to.

I step forward, my boots pressing down slow against the old tile. Every creak in the floor, every shadow on the wall feels too sharp, like the building's holding its breath.

My hand brushes the stairwell door—it's ice cold.

Another creak from below.

Whoever's down there... they're not in a hurry. That's the part that chills me the most.

I push the door open and descend.

One step.
Two.
The air down here shifts—damp, metallic. Like rust and old secrets. The kind of air you don't breathe too deep if you know what's good for you.

My flashlight beam cuts the dark in a narrow line, sweeping past stacked chairs, boxes, and long-forgotten files. This place hasn't seen daylight in years. And yet... the faint sound of movement echoes just ahead.

"Andre?" I whisper again.

No answer.

The basement corridor splits at the end—left toward the evidence locker, right toward the old boiler room. I hear something metallic clatter down the right path.

So I move left.

I need to stay ahead of whoever's playing games with me.

That's when I spot it.

A shoe. Half-hidden beneath a pile of old blankets near the janitor's sink.

Deadly Oath

I kneel, peeling back the fabric, heart thudding like a war drum.

It's Andre.

Lying on his side, unconscious—or worse. There's blood near his temple, and one of his hands is duct-taped to a pipe.

I press two fingers to his neck.

Pulse—weak, but there.

He stirs.

"Stanley," he croaks, barely audible. "They knew I was coming. It's... someone we trust..."

"Don't talk," I whisper. "I've got you."

I start to reach for my radio when a noise cuts through the dark—high-pitched, electric, *close*.

The monitor upstairs isn't the only one playing.

A second screen flickers to life in the far corner of the basement, mounted above the boiler tank. It casts a sickly blue light across the cement wall.

And it's not playing security footage this time.

It's a *live* feed.

From inside the precinct.

The main lobby.

Someone in uniform walks past the camera, then turns—and stares straight into the lens.

My breath catches.

It's *me*.

But I'm standing down here.

A chill spiders up my neck.

On the screen, "Stanley" walks to the front desk, nods at the officer, then disappears from view.

"What the hell..." I mutter.

Andre groans behind me. "It's not just murder anymore..."

"What is it then?" I ask, eyes still glued to the screen.

His answer comes out in a whisper, just before he loses consciousness again:

"It's infiltration."

The feed cuts to black.

And from the shadows just beyond the boiler room—

A voice echoes.

Familiar. Calm. Almost... friendly.

"Detective Stanley," it says.

"I've been waiting for you."

Chapter 48

That creaking noise isn't just the building settling. It's deliberate, slow, like someone's walking away or waiting.

I move toward the stairwell, each step deliberate, my Glock raised. The fluorescent lights above me flicker once more, then cut out completely, plunging the hallway into shadows thick as smoke. The only light now spills from that monitor in the records room, still looping the grainy footage of Angela's body and the man stepping over her.

My footsteps echo.

Gun tight in my hands, I reach the door to the stairwell.

Another creak.

Then a metallic clang.

I twist the knob and push the door open.

The smell hits me first—bleach and copper. My stomach clenches. I've smelled this before.

Blood.

I move down the narrow concrete steps, the air colder with each descent. My flashlight beam slices through the dark. The walls are unfinished—pipes exposed, one of them dripping.

At the bottom of the stairs, the basement door hangs open on one hinge.

Inside, it's silent.

No humming from the heaters. No backup generators. Just silence and darkness.

Then my light hits something.

Shoes.

Black loafers. Lying sideways like someone ran out of them in a rush.

I step closer. My beam travels upward—

A pair of legs.

A body.

Slumped against the boiler.

"Andre?" I choke out.

I move in fast, heart jackhammering against my ribs.

It's him.

Detective Andre Andre.

Face swollen. Bruised. Tape over his mouth. Hands zip-tied behind the boiler pipe.

But he's alive.

His eyes lock with mine—vast and urgent—and he starts shaking his head violently.

My stomach drops.

He's trying to warn me.

But it's too late.

I hear it.

Behind me.

The softest inhale of breath.

And then—

A whisper:

"Detective Stanley… you've finally caught up."

I spin around—

But I see only the outline of a mask before the pipe connects with my skull.

Everything goes black.

Chapter 49

I still feel the sting in my ribs as I shift in the conference room chair. The bruises from last night pulse with every breath I take. That shadowy figure—whatever the hell they were—caught me off guard in the precinct basement, cracked a pipe across my shoulder, and damn near took my head off. I'm lucky to be walking today. My partner, Andre, wasn't so fortunate. I found him with tape over his mouth, zip-tied at the wrists, his face puffed like a melon. We haven't spoken much about it. We don't need to. The silence says enough.

We're sitting in the cold, corporate lobby of Lance & Associates by nine a.m., waiting to peel back another layer of this case. Andre's eyes the receptionist, as if she's hiding something. Me—I'm watching every hallway.

The owner bursts through the double doors. He's tall, wiry, and overly cheerful for someone whose staff is dropping like flies.

"Good morning, Detectives Stanley and Detective Andre," he says, extending his hand. "I'm Lance. Any questions you have should be answered before you leave here today. Follow me."

We trail behind him like shadows slipping down a hallway and into a sterile, glass-paneled conference room.

"Can I offer you something to drink?" he asks.

"No," I say, deadpan. "We're just here for answers."

He snorts out a laugh, trying to break the tension. It doesn't work.

I slide a photo across the table. Cindy. Her eyes stare back at Lance from beneath the glossy surface. "She worked here, didn't she?"

Lance stiffens. "Yes. She was our Director of Human Resources. She recruited candidates."

I slide the next photo. "What about this woman?"

"That's Fatima. She worked in HR, too. And Angela," he adds as I slide over the third photo, "was promoted right after Cindy's death."

Andre takes over, laying down three more photos like playing cards in a deadly hand: Katie, Trina, Rebecca.

"They all worked here?" he asks.

"Yes. All HR assistants or generalists. They attended the same recruitment fairs."

Andre leans in. "Your employees are being hunted. Do you know why?"

"No," Lance says. "None of them mentioned any threats."

"Were there others who attended those fairs?" I ask.

"One—Becky. She just returned from vacation. You can talk to her."

He makes a call. Moments later, Becky walks in.

Her eyes are tired. Her posture was defensive.

"There's not much I can tell you," she snaps. "It's my first day back."

"You're the last one left," Andre tells her. "Everyone else is dead."

Her face falls.

We question her, warn her, and assign a patrol. As we exit, Becky returns to her desk—oblivious to what's stalking her.

Chapter 50

Later that night. I'm back at the desk, trying to shake the image of my partner's swollen face. My ribs ache. I'm popping ibuprofen like candy. But something keeps clawing at me—something about Becky. I can't sleep, so I drive back to her neighborhood.

Her home is quiet. A cruiser is parked outside. Good.

Becky's inside, trying to resume an everyday life— cooking dinner, peeling potatoes, doing laundry. She's trying to forget the weight of our warning. But that shadow I saw in the basement? I've got a sick feeling it hasn't forgotten her.

Then it happens.

A scream cuts through the night like a razor. I'm out of the car and charging up her porch with Andre on my heels.

I shoulder the door open just in time to see her fall to the floor, blood pouring from her shoulder. A man in a wig looms over her with a cleaver, ready to strike again.

I draw. Fire. The blast lights up the room. The intruder stumbles back, crashing onto the tile.

Becky screams, clutching her wound. Blood everywhere.

We rush to her, applying towels, pressure, anything to keep her awake. Outside, sirens blare, red and blue lights reflecting across neighboring windows. Piper, Becky's neighbor, is already out front, screaming her name.

Paramedics arrive and haul the attacker up onto a stretcher. But something's off.

Andre enters the scene just as the paramedics start peeling off the disguise.

"What's the situation?" he asks.

"This isn't just a man," the medic says. "This is a madman."

They rip off the mask. Underneath is a stocking cap.

Then—confirmation.

Andre's voice drops cold. "That's no stranger. That's Robert Samuel Brown. Sam."

The name hangs in the air like a cloud of smoke.

Sam.

The same man we met at Elijah's shooting. The same man who got into a fight at that party, like he belonged there—the same shadow in the precinct basement.

He was right under our noses the whole time.

But then, Sam moves.

His hand shoots out and grabs Becky's ankle when she's helped over to a stretcher. She screams. The gurney jolts. He yanks her down.

I don't hesitate. I fire again—one shot to the arm. Robert hits the wall, gasping, sliding down to the floor. But even as the paramedics drag him away—bloodied, gasping—his eyes are open.

Watching her.

Watching me.

And smiling.

Chapter 51

The moment I pull up to the office building, I know something's wrong.

It's too quiet. No lobby music. No secretary at the front desk. Just the low, buzzing hum of fluorescent lights and a faint echo down the marble hallway. My ribs still ache from the ambush in the precinct basement, but I press on. I'm here to follow up with Becky. She returned to work this morning, and something's been gnawing at me ever since I saw the terror in her eyes yesterday.

I push the stairwell door open and ascend quietly, each step heavy beneath my boots.

Then I hear it.

A scuffle. Papers rustling. A faint gasp.

I edge closer, careful not to reveal myself.

Through a crack in the doorway, I see Becky stepping into her office, her heels crunching on paper scattered across the floor. Mail is piled like bricks on her desk. She hesitates—eyes darting to the hallway—then walks to her chair.

Suddenly, she freezes.

Her eyes lock on something in the hallway. She moves toward the door cautiously, but by the time she looks, the figure is gone.

That's when I see it—just a sliver of movement, a flicker of black disappearing around the corner.

She bolts. I follow at a distance.

She flies down the stairwell like she's being hunted. And she is. Just as she reaches the ground floor, I stop dead in my tracks.

He's here.

The masked killer.

He's standing right by the exit—tall, still, like he's been waiting—and then, total darkness.

The lights cut out. Electricity hums and dies.

I press my back against the wall, heart hammering. I can't move yet—not until I know where Robert is.

I hear her breathing first—shallow, frantic. Then the slap of her shoes on tile as she runs.

Becky.

She's heading for the elevator, mashing the button with a desperate rhythm. I inch forward, hugging the shadows.

The lights flicker back on, and he moves.

He's heading toward her.

I see his hand, gloved, steady, reaching into his coat.

Come on. Come on.

The elevator dings.

She dives inside just as the doors begin to shut. Her attacker lunges, but it's too late. The doors close in his face.

I can't blow my cover yet.

I slip into the nearest office and move toward the stairwell. I hear a scream from upstairs.

I'm coming, Becky.

By the time I reach the top, the scream dies into a muffled whimper. I hear crashing, furniture being overturned. Then silence.

I'm too late.

No—I won't accept that.

I inch forward again, Glock drawn. I round the corner just in time to hear another crash.

She's alive. Fighting.

I reach the reception area and see Becky—blood on her sleeve, wide-eyed, breathing hard—standing over a body near her office door. The killer's down. She hesitates, steps over him.

"Don't go near that body," I whisper to myself.

He springs up.

She screams and bolts for the stairs. I raise my gun, but Robert is already gone—vanished back into the maze of offices and exits.

I don't chase. Not yet.

Because I hear something else.

A voice—male, hushed, low. Coming from the breakroom down the hall.

I stalk toward it, silent as breath, peering through the cracked door.

There's a phone on the counter. It's on speaker.

A man's voice filters through the static.

"You did well," he says. "We'll be back for her."

My pulse surges.

Then another voice. Familiar. Calm. Controlled.

"We had her. She got lucky. We won't next time."

I know that voice.

Ron. The corrections officer.

The one who gave us nothing when we questioned him about Robert.

And now he's talking to someone. Someone else who's out there—free.

"I'll open the doors at 12:30," Ron says. "No one will see it coming."

Then—click. The call ends.

I take a step back, heart hammering like a war drum.

Robert Brown—Sam—isn't alone. He has help.

And if Ron is opening doors, then the nightmare isn't over.

It's just beginning.

I pull out my phone to call Andre—

But I stop cold.

The elevator dings behind me.

I turn slowly.

And standing there, just a few feet away, is Robert.

No mask.

No disguise.

Smiling.

Alive.

Chapter 52

I'm halfway done with my coffee when I see the news van. Big, white, with *Headline News* splashed across the side in bold red letters. The kind of van you only see when someone dies—or escapes.

It screeches to a halt outside the jailhouse gates. I step away from my unmarked car and move toward the sidewalk, heart already thudding harder than it should. The back door bursts open, and out jumps Kristi Bell in her perfectly pressed blazer and disaster-hungry eyes. Her cameraman is right behind her, already hoisting the rig onto his shoulder.

She spots the building, the camera goes live, and that voice—clean, cool, and sharp as a razor—cuts through the air:

"This is Kristi Bell reporting live outside the facility where Robert Samuel Brown, the man accused in the Ring Zone killings, was being held after his arrest."

I stiffen.

Was being held?

The anchor back in the studio sounds shaken, fumbling to silence the basketball game they've interrupted. The screen above the van on the building's exterior flips to live feed. Kristi turns back to the camera, and her expression hardens.

"Sources have confirmed to me exclusively—he's out."

That's all she says.

Then the screen cuts back to the anchor, stunned into silence.

My heart drops.

The front gate of the jail is sealed. The yard is quiet. No alarms, no sirens. But Kristi doesn't speak in riddles. Not unless she's been handed something on record. If she's saying he's out... something's happened inside they don't want us to see yet.

My phone buzzes.

Unknown Number.

No message. No voicemail. Just that subtle pulse of warning.

And then, like a scene from a movie I've seen before but never wanted to live through—

I hear it.

Screaming.

Not from the street.

From the second floor of the hospital, across the road.

Becky.

Her voice shreds through the windowpane like glass. I look up and see her silhouette—wild, flailing, ripping at the blankets. Her sister wraps her in her arms, rocking, trying to calm her.

"It's okay," the sister repeats. "It's okay."

But it's not. Becky's eyes are locked on the television mounted in her room. The same feed from outside. Kristi Bell's report.

I start running. Toward the hospital, toward the truth I'm not ready to hear.

Because if Robert's out...

Someone let him out.

And that means someone *inside* is helping him.

But just as I reach the emergency room doors, a hand clamps down on my shoulder.

I spin.

It's not a nurse.

Not an officer.

It's a man in a gray jumpsuit and a smirk I've seen once before—burned into a crime scene photo from Angela Dorsey's apartment.

"Detective Stanley," he says softly, voice smooth as silk.

"You're already too late."

Author Biography – Wendell Peeples

Wendell Peeples is an American suspense and thriller author whose storytelling dives deep into the darkest corners of human nature. Known for his cinematic writing style and gripping realism, Peeples crafts stories that blend psychological tension, social commentary, and emotional depth. His ability to capture both the grit and fragility of life has earned him recognition among readers who crave stories that stay with them long after the final page.

A native of Detroit, Michigan, Wendell Peeples grew up surrounded by the pulse of city life—its beauty, its struggle, and its endless stories. From an early age, he was drawn to mysteries, true crime, and the hidden motives that drive people to cross moral boundaries. These early fascinations became the cornerstone of his writing career. His characters are layered, his plots unpredictable, and his dialogue sharp with authenticity.

Peeples' debut novel, **Deadly Oath**, established him as a fresh and fearless voice in modern suspense fiction. The book centers on Detective Stanley, a man haunted by his past and trapped in a labyrinth of lies, corruption, and revenge. Written in first-person, present-tense, *Deadly Oath* draws readers directly into the detective's fractured mind, forcing them to experience every heartbeat of danger, every flicker of doubt, and every chilling revelation.

What sets Peeples apart is his ability to merge psychological realism with cinematic storytelling. He paints each scene with precision—dark alleys, rain-slicked streets, and quiet rooms where secrets whisper louder than words. His prose is alive with tension, and his cliffhangers are the kind that make readers lose sleep just to turn one more page.

Beyond his mastery of suspense, Wendell Peeples explores themes that cut to the core of society—racial discrimination, trauma, justice, and the complexity of human morality. His writing challenges readers to confront uncomfortable truths while keeping them riveted by the relentless pace of his plots. Each chapter feels like a heartbeat in the shadow of something inevitable, a style that has become his signature.

When he's not writing, Peeples draws inspiration from music, photography, and the rhythm of everyday people and places. He believes stories should reflect the world as it is—messy, unpredictable, and painfully real. His dedication to truth in storytelling has earned him praise not just for his narrative talent but for his emotional honesty as a writer.

Now, Wendell Peeples returns with his chilling second novel, *I'll Get You Back*—a relentless psychological thriller that explores vengeance, obsession, and the thin line between justice and madness. With his trademark suspense and cinematic flair, Peeples once again proves his mastery at weaving fear, emotion, and humanity into a narrative that grips the soul and won't let go.

I'll Get You Back cements Wendell Peeples' place as a powerful voice in the genre—a storyteller who doesn't just write thrillers, but experiences them with his readers.